THE SIMON & SCHUSTER
POCKET BOOK OF
CHESS

THE SIMON & SCHUSTER POCKET BOOK OF
CHESS

RAYMOND
KEENE

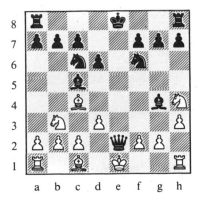

Simon and Schuster Books for Young Readers
Published by Simon & Schuster Inc., New York

The publishers would like to thank David Levy for his assistance
in acting as a specialist editor on this book.

The author would like to thank Dr. Jacqueline Levy for her assistance
in researching this book.

**SIMON AND SCHUSTER
BOOKS FOR YOUNG READERS**
Simon & Schuster Building
Rockefeller Center
1230 Avenue of the Americas
New York, New York 10020

SIMON AND SCHUSTER BOOKS FOR YOUNG READERS
is a trademark of Simon & Schuster Inc.
Originally published in Great Britain by Kingfisher Books
Edited by Jacqui Bailey and Jackie Gaff
Designed by David Jefferis
Manufactured in Spain

10 9 8 7 6 5 4 3 2 1

10 9 8 7 6 5 4   (pbk.)

Library of Congress Cataloging-in-Publication Data

Keene, Raymond D.
  Pocket book of chess.

  Includes index.
  Summary: Describes the game of chess, from the basic
moves to strategies for attack and defense, with
chapters on the history of the game, great champions,
competitions, and computer chess.
  1. Chess—Juvenile literature. [1. Chess]
I. Title.
GV1446.K43 1989 794.1'2 88-30555
ISBN 0-671-67923-6
ISBN 0-671-67924-4 (pbk.)

Contents

♟ Introduction

Chess is one of the world's oldest war games. It was invented in northern India some time before A.D. 600, and the original pieces were based on the infantry, cavalry, elephants, and chariots of the ancient Indian army. These troops were led onto the chessboard by the king and his chief minister, the vizier.

From India, chess spread to central Asia, China, Persia (modern-day Iran), and Europe, reaching Spain by the middle of the 11th century. In the West the design of the chess pieces changed to reflect the society of medieval Europe. The king remained, and the pawns were still the foot soldiers, but the elephant was replaced by the bishop, the horse became the knight, and the chariot was changed into the rook, or castle. Finally, the vizier became the queen, and at the end of the 15th century a change in the rules of the game made the queen the most powerful piece on the chessboard. This is the version of chess that is played worldwide today, and which is officially recognized by the international ruling body of chess, **FIDE** (Fédération Internationale des Échecs).

King

Queen

Bishop

Rook

Pawn

Knight

◀▲ **The Isle of Lewis pieces** shown opposite are from the oldest-known complete chess set. They date from the 12th century A.D. and are probably Viking in origin. The pieces on this page are from a Staunton chess set. Designed by Nathaniel Cook in 1839, this is the set used for normal play.

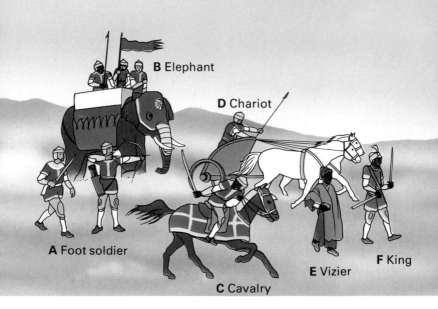

B Elephant

D Chariot

A Foot soldier

C Cavalry

E Vizier

F King

Until the present century, chess was regarded primarily as a game for the wealthy and leisured classes in society. Today chess has a much broader appeal and is played by millions of people throughout the world. It is the national sport in the Soviet Union, where it is more popular than soccer. Indeed, Soviet chess players have dominated world chess since the 1940s, although their superiority is fast being challenged by Britain, which is now established as the second strongest chess nation in the world.

Among all board games, chess seems to possess the perfect blend of strategy and tactics. Compare it with, say, checkers (nearly all tactics), or with the Japanese game Go (nearly all strategy), and both these games are lacking in balance. Chess also has the advantage of its finely differentiated playing pieces. They are not merely rounded lumps of wood or stone but individuals, each with its own power and attributes. It is easy to identify with one's chess pieces — losing a game of checkers never results in the same sense of deep personal loss that one has when a king is checkmated. Chess is a game that involves the ego completely.

Chess combines elements of both art and science. Analyzing a

A Pawn **B** Bishop **C** Knight **D** Rook **E** Queen **F** King

▲ **Invented in northern India** some time before A.D. 600, the original chess pieces were based on the ancient Indian army. Over the centuries, once the game reached the West, the design of the pieces changed to reflect the society of medieval Europe. In the Soviet Union, where chess is very popular, the bishop is still known by its traditional name of elephant (*slon*).

chess game is primarily an exercise in logic, yet arriving at a beautiful mating attack or a profound strategical position can bring a genuine sense of creative satisfaction. There is also the competitive aspect of the game. Chess is not a solitary exercise, like solving a crossword puzzle, but a battle between two individuals, a struggle of mind and will.

Above all, chess provides a sense of continuity with the past — of belonging to a great chess-playing family extending through hundreds of years and embracing all nations. In this book you will find games played over a century ago that still arouse admiration in those who play through them today. Perhaps one day, my readers who are now taking up chess will find some of their own efforts gracing the literature of this fascinating game.

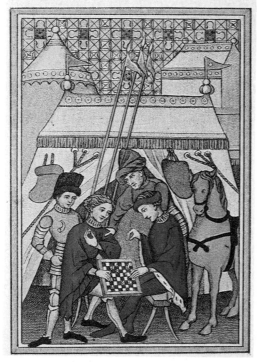

From India, chess spread to central Asia, China, Persia (modern-day Iran), and Europe, reaching Spain by the middle of the 11th century. The illustration above is from the first European work on chess, supervised by King Alfonso the Wise in the late 13th century. Until the present century chess was considered a game for the wealthy and leisured classes. The engraving left is medieval, while the painting opposite dates from the 17th century.

Chess sets have varied enormously over the ages. The exquisitely carved ivory pieces opposite are from a Chinese set made around 1850. The inlaid wooden chessboard and delicate pieces above date from the late 17th century and are said to have belonged to the diarist Samuel Pepys. But the amusing pieces below are 20th century creations!

1: Rules of the Game

To learn to play chess, all you need is a chess set and a friend who either knows how to play or wants to learn with you. Every chess set has two armies, one light-colored and one dark-colored, and each army consists of 16 pieces — one king, one queen, two bishops, two knights, two rooks, and eight pawns.

The chessboard is your battlefield. It is divided into 64 squares, arranged in eight rows of eight. The squares are alternately light and dark (usually white and black) and the board is always positioned with a light square at the lower right-hand corner facing each player.

The board is further divided into the queen's side and the king's side, also called the queen's flank or queen's wing and the king's flank or king's wing. The bishop, knight, and rook nearest to the king are called the king's bishop, king's knight, and king's rook. Those nearest to the queen are the queen's bishop, queen's knight, and queen's rook.

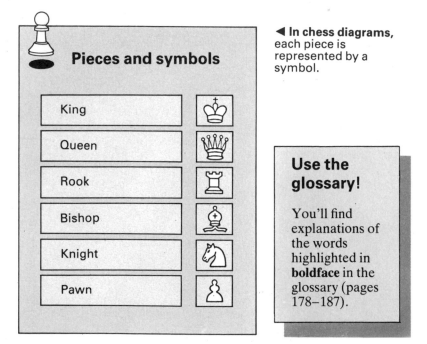

Pieces and symbols

◀ **In chess diagrams,** each piece is represented by a symbol.

King	♔
Queen	♕
Rook	♖
Bishop	♗
Knight	♘
Pawn	♙

Use the glossary!

You'll find explanations of the words highlighted in **boldface** in the glossary (pages 178–187).

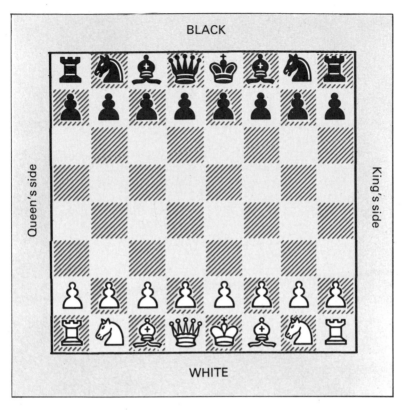

The diagram above shows how the chess pieces are placed at the beginning of a game. The queen always starts the game on her own color square — White's queen begins on a white square, and Black's queen on a black square. In chess diagrams Black's pieces always start at the top of the board and White's pieces are always at the bottom.

Traditionally, the two chess armies are referred to as White and Black, but chess sets are just as likely to be colored white and red, beige and brown, or white

▲ **A chess game always opens** with the chess pieces in this position. Make sure the square at the lower right-hand corner facing each player is light-colored as here.

and green. Very elaborate multicolored sets have been made to represent Napoleon's army fighting against the Duke of Wellington's forces, for instance, or opposing political parties, but the chess sets used for friendly and tournament play are normally of a simple design (see page 7).

Playing the Game

Your aim in a chess game is to trap your opponent's king. This situation is called **checkmate**, or mate.

To deliver checkmate you must make a move that both attacks the enemy king and prevents your opponent from making a reply that would remove it from attack. If you checkmate your opponent, the game is over and you have won.

You will also win if your opponent decides to **resign**, or withdraw from the game. This might happen if your opponent is sure that his or her position is hopeless and that it is only a matter of time before you deliver checkmate.

If it is not possible for either side to force checkmate, the game is drawn. In this case there is no outright winner and the honors are shared. This might happen, for example, if each player has only a king remaining on the board.

There are other ways of drawing a game. If both players think that neither of them has much chance of winning, they can agree to a draw. Or a game can be drawn by **stalemate** (see pages 61–63).

At the start of a game White is always the first to move. Players must take turns to make a move and they cannot refuse to do so.

Each chess piece is allowed to move in a particular way. The pawn can move forward, for instance, but not backward. Players are allowed to move only their own pieces, and two pieces cannot be placed on the same square at the same time.

To **capture** (or take) a piece, you must move one of your pieces so that it lands on a square containing one of your opponent's pieces. The captured enemy piece is then taken from the board and removed from the game. (The only ex-ception to this way of capturing is the **en passant** move, which is explained on page 31.)

It is considered good manners in chess to move a piece once you have touched it. This is called the **touch-move rule** and in competition games it is com-pulsory. In friendly games you will often find players who don't insist on this rule, but it is a good habit to avoid touching a piece unless you are sure that you want to move it.

If you want to adjust one of your pieces because it is not positioned correctly, in the center of its square, you should first say "*j'adoube*," which is French for "I adjust."

▲ **When playing chess, avoid** touching a piece unless you intend to move it. This is compulsory in competition chess.

◀ **The best way to learn chess** — and the most enjoyable — is by practicing with a friend who either knows how to play or wants to learn with you.

2: Chess Notation

In chess, notation is a system of abbreviation that makes it easier to discuss and record the moves of a game. It's a shorthand way of describing what is happening on the chessboard.

You'll find it useful to take a few moments to learn chess notation now, before reading any further, as otherwise it may be difficult for you to understand much of what follows. You will also find chess notation very important when you want to read other chess books or magazines, or to follow the chess columns that appear in many newspapers.

The modern method of recording chess games is called **algebraic notation**. It is the only system officially recognized by **FIDE**, the International Chess Federation. Algebraic notation is based on a simple grid system of eight letters and eight numbers.

The chessboard is divided into eight vertical columns called **files**, each of which is identified by one of the letters **a** to **h**. The file to the far left of White's side is always the a-file, so Black's a-file is always on the far right.

The eight horizontal columns are called **ranks**, and each rank is given one of the numbers **1** to **8**. The rank nearest to White's side of the board is always 1, while that nearest to Black's side is 8.

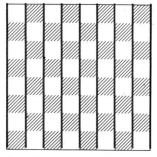

FILES

◀ ▼ **The vertical columns of the** chessboard are called files and the horizontal ones, ranks. Each file is identified by one of the letters **a** to **h**, and each rank by one of the numbers **1** to **8**.

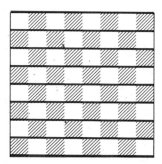

RANKS

BLACK

	a	b	c	d	e	f	g	h	
8	a8	b8	c8	d8	e8	f8	g8	h8	8
7	a7	b7	c7	d7	e7	f7	g7	h7	7
6	a6	b6	c6	d6	e6	f6	g6	h6	6
5	a5	b5	c5	d5	e5	f5	g5	h5	5
4	a4	b4	c4	d4	e4	f4	g4	h4	4
3	a3	b3	c3	d3	e3	f3	g3	h3	3
2	a2	b2	c2	d2	e2	f2	g2	h2	2
1	a1	b1	c1	d1	e1	f1	g1	h1	1
	a	b	c	d	e	f	g	h	

WHITE

▲ **Algebraic notation is based** on a simple grid system of eight letters and eight numbers.

You can see above how the eight squares in the a-file are called a1, a2, a3, a4, a5, a6, a7 and a8. The letter *a* in each case indicates that the square is on the a-file, while the numbers 1 to 8 refer to its rank.

So, every square on the chessboard can be identified by a simple reference code, made up of a letter from **a** to **h**, followed by a number from **1** to **8**. In the starting position, for example, before any moves have been made, White's king is on the square e1 and his queen is on d1. On the other side, Black's king is on e8 and her queen on d8.

You'll find that using algebraic notation will make chess a lot easier. Instead of saying "White's queen is moving three squares in front and one to the right of Black's queen's bishop," you can now simply say "White's queen is moving to d5."

♔	–	King	– K
♕	–	Queen	– Q
♖	–	Rook	– R
♗	–	Bishop	– B
♘	–	Knight	– N

◀ **In chess notation,** each chess piece is identified by a single capital letter. The exception is the pawn. The knight is represented by N to avoid confusion with the K for king.

In chess notation, each of the chess pieces, apart from the pawn, is identified by a capital letter (see above). It isn't necessary to use P for pawns, since it is enough to describe the square from which the pawn came and the one to which it is moving. The pawns are described according to the file they occupy. Thus, at the start of a game, the pawn in front of the king is called the e-pawn and the pawn in front of the queen, the d-pawn. If a pawn moves to a different file later in the game it changes its name.

There are different forms of algebraic notation and the one used throughout this book is called "full algebraic." When recording a move, the letter for the chess piece is written first (unless the piece is a pawn) and followed by the square that the piece occupied before the move.

Next, if the move is not a **capture**, a short – (dash) is written. This means that the piece is moving to a vacant square. If the

move is a capture, a × (cross) is written to signify that the piece is moving to an occupied square. You will find that some people prefer to use a : (colon) instead of the × to indicate a capture. To the right of the – or the × is written the square to which the piece is moving. Finally, if the move results in **check**, a + (plus) is added.

White's moves are always recorded first, and then Black's. The moves are usually written in columns, but sometimes they are given horizontally, across the page.

All this will become a little clearer if you use your chess set to try out the examples that follow. At this stage don't worry about the rules governing the way the different chess pieces move — just see how the algebraic notation for the moves relates to the location of the pieces in the diagrams.

The first game is known as Fool's Mate, and it is the quickest way possible to lose a game!

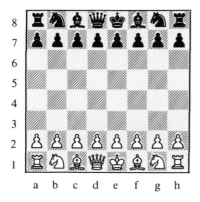

Follow these moves from the starting position shown above.

White	Black
1. g2 – g4	e7 – e5

White begins the game by advancing his pawn on the g-file from g2 to g4. This is White's first move and so the number 1 appears to the left.

Black replies by advancing her e-pawn from e7 to e5. The board below shows the position after these first moves.

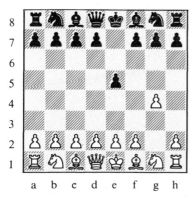

White's second move (hence the number 2 on the left) is to advance his pawn from f2 to the f3 square.

2. f2 – f3	Qd8 – h4
	checkmate

Black responds by bringing out her queen from d8 to h4. The board below illustrates the position of the chess pieces after this second move by Black.

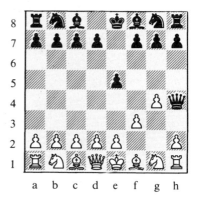

Because the black queen on h4 is now attacking the white king on e1, the white king is in **check**. The only vacant square to which White's king can try to move is f2, but f2 is also under attack from Black's queen on h4.

White cannot escape from the attack by moving his king, nor can he **capture** Black's queen or move another piece to block the attack. White has been **checkmated** and the game is over. Black has won.

Scholar's Mate

Here is another example of a chess game and its notation. Try to remember what happens in this game, because the moves will almost certainly be attempted against you. More beginners have lost to Scholar's Mate than to any other play.

Begin by setting up your chessboard and pieces in the starting position (see page 15).

White	Black
1. e2 – e4	e7 – e5

White starts the game by advancing his e-pawn two squares, from e2 to e4. Black responds in the same way, advancing her e-pawn from e7 to e5.

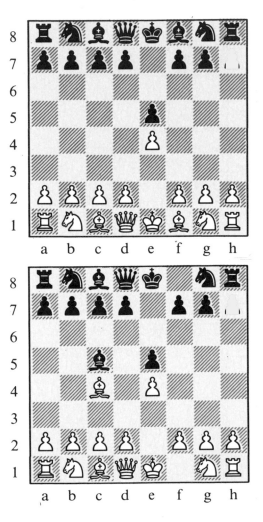

2. Bf1 – c4   Bf8 – c5

White's second move is to bring out his bishop from f1 to c4. Black responds in parrot fashion, moving her bishop from f8 to c5.

3. Qd1 – h5   Nb8 – c6

White's third move is to advance his queen from d1 to h5. Black replies by moving her knight from b8 to c6.

4. Qh5 × f7
   checkmate

White advances his queen from h5 and **captures** the black f-pawn, removing it from the game and taking its place on f7. From its new square, the white queen delivers **checkmate**, aided along the a2–g8 diagonal by the white bishop on c4. White has won the game.

Other Symbols

A few additional symbols are used in chess notation, to comment on moves and to describe special moves. For example, writing an exclamation mark after a move indicates that it is a good move; a question mark means a weak move. The most important of these symbols are shown below.

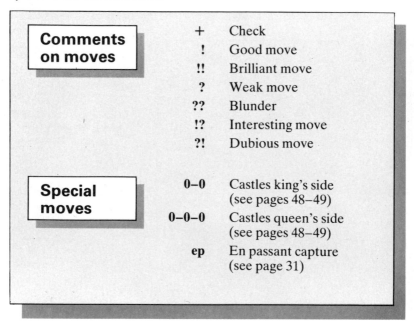

Comments on moves	+	Check
	!	Good move
	!!	Brilliant move
	?	Weak move
	??	Blunder
	!?	Interesting move
	?!	Dubious move
Special moves	0–0	Castles king's side (see pages 48–49)
	0–0–0	Castles queen's side (see pages 48–49)
	ep	En passant capture (see page 31)

In competition chess each player uses a piece of paper called a **score sheet** to record all the moves made during the game. Some players also like to write on their score sheets the amount of thinking time they take at various stages of the game (or even after every move).

The illustration opposite shows the score sheets used by Boris Spassky (U.S.S.R.) and Bobby Fischer (U.S.A.) for their game played during the 1970 Chess Olympiad at Siegen, West Germany. Spassky won this particular game, and if you look closely you'll see that his score sheet (the one above) is uniformly neat. Fischer's writing, on the other hand, becomes more and more messy during the later stages of the game, when his position is deteriorating.

XIX. Schach Olympiade

Vor/Finalgruppe: A
Runde: 6
Partie-Nr.: 133
Brett: 1

Weiß: Spassky
Nation: UdSSR

Schwarz: Fischer
Nation: USA

Weiß:	Schwarz:	Weiß:	Schwarz:
d2 - d4	Kg8 - f6	21 Le1 - e2	c5 : d4
2 c2 - c4	g7 - g6	22 c3 : d4	b6 - b5
3 Kb1 - c3	d7 - d5	23 Kg8 - e3	Cc8 : d4
4 c4 : d5	Kf6 : d5	24 Ke3 - g5	Cd4 : f2
5 e2 - e4	Kd5 : c3	25 Mf1 : f2	Kd5 - d6
6 b2 : c3	Cf8 - g7	26 Le1 - e1	Ld6 - b6
7 Lf1 - c4	c7 - c5	27 Kg5 - e4	Ld6 - d4
8 Kg1 - e2	Kb8 - c6	28 Ke4 - f6+	Kg8 - h8
9 Lc1 - e3	0 - 0	29 Le3 - e6	Qd4 - d6
10 0 - 0	Qd8 - c7	30 Le6 - e4	Ld8 - f8
11 Lc1 - c1	Mf8 - d8	31 g4 - g5	Ld6 - d2
12 h2 - h3	b7 - b6	32 Kf6 - f1	Qb6 - c7
13 f2 - f4	b7 - c6	33 Kf6 : d7	Le7 : d7
14 Qd1 - e1	Kc6 ...	34 Ke4 - d4	Lf8 - d8
15 c4 - d5	...	35 Rh8 : g8	R... : h6
16 g2 - g4	...		
17 Kd5 - e7	Cc8 ...		
18 Ke7 - g5	...		
19 Ce5 : f7			
20 Ce5 - f2			

Other Forms of Chess Notation

Another form of **algebraic notation** is quicker to write but slightly more difficult for a beginner to learn. This system does not normally indicate the square from which a piece moves, nor does it include the – sign for a move that isn't a **capture**. In addition, some players who use this method of notation also omit the × (or :) symbol used in full algebraic to indicate a capture.

To see what short algebraic notation looks like, compare the two methods given below of recording Scholar's Mate, the game introduced on pages 22–23.

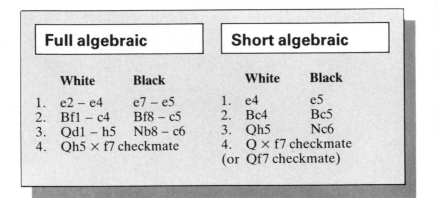

Full algebraic			**Short algebraic**	
White	**Black**		**White**	**Black**
1. e2 – e4	e7 – e5		1. e4	e5
2. Bf1 – c4	Bf8 – c5		2. Bc4	Bc5
3. Qd1 – h5	Nb8 – c6		3. Qh5	Nc6
4. Qh5 × f7 checkmate			4. Q × f7 checkmate	
			(or Qf7 checkmate)	

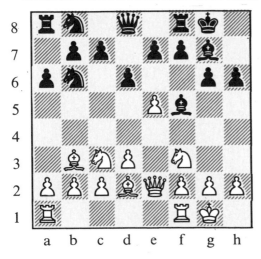

◄ **In order to avoid** ambiguities that can arise when using short algebraic notation, another letter or number is sometimes added when recording a move. Here, for example, White has rooks on a1 and f1, both of which can move to e1. The two rook moves would be distinguished by writing Rae1 or Rfe1.

When using the short form of algebraic notation you will some-times find it necessary to add another letter or number to record a move, in order to resolve an ambiguity. On the chessboard at the bottom of the facing page, for example, White has rooks on a1 and f1, either of which could move to e1. In short algebraic notation, moving the rook from a1 to e1 would be written Rae1, while the other rook move to e1 would be recorded as Rfe1. Similarly, Black has two knights that can both move to d7 — one on b8 and one on b6. The two moves would be distinguished by writing . . . N8d7 and . . . N6d7.

Note that in both short and full algebraic, the three dots before each of the previous moves indicate that they are Black's moves. The dots show that White's move, which is always recorded first, has been omitted.

Review quiz 1

Here is a simple chess game for you to work through, so that you can test your understanding of the way full algebraic notation works.

Set up your chessboard and pieces in the starting position (see page 15) and play through the moves listed below. After eight moves each, by White and by Black, your chess pieces should be in the position illustrated on page 28.

	White	Black
1.	d2 – d4	Ng8 – f6
2.	c2 – c4	g7 – g6
3.	Nb1 – c3	Bf8 – g7
4.	e2 – e4	d7 – d6
5.	Ng1 – f3	Nb8 – c6
6.	Bc1 – g5	e7 – e5
7.	d4 × e5	d6 × e5
8.	Qd1 × d8+	Ke8 × d8

3: How Pieces Move

The Pawn

Pawns are the foot soldiers of the chess army and each player has eight of them. Throughout the long history of the game their basic moves have changed very little.

The pawns are the least powerful pieces on the chessboard, because they are very restricted in their movements. They cannot move backward or sideways. Unless taking another piece, they must move forward.

Usually pawns advance only one square at a time, but there is an exception to this rule. At the start of the game, players are allowed to move their pawns either one or two squares forward — any pawn still on its starting square can advance one or two squares. After this first move, the pawns are restricted to moving one square at a time.

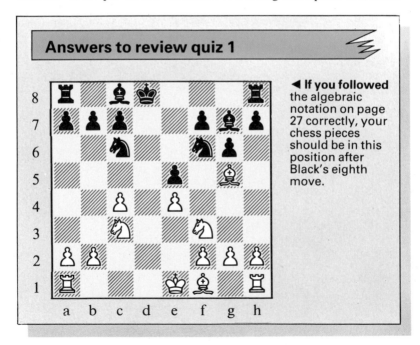

Answers to review quiz 1

◀ **If you followed** the algebraic notation on page 27 correctly, your chess pieces should be in this position after Black's eighth move.

▲ On its first move of the game (A), each pawn is allowed to advance either one or two squares. After this, pawns can move only one square at a time (B).

► Pawns capture diagonally. Here, the white pawn on d4 can take the black pawn on e5, or vice versa, depending on whether it is White's turn to move, or Black's.

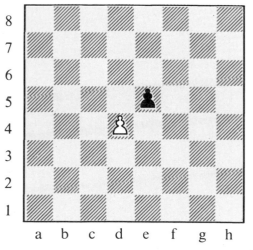

Unlike all the other chess pieces, pawns do not **capture** in the same way that they move. Although they normally move forward, they take other pieces by moving one square diagonally. You can see an example of this on the chessboard above — if it were White's turn to move, his pawn on d4 could take Black's pawn on e5.

29

Here are the first few moves of a game in which both players move only their pawns.

Set up your chessboard and pieces in the starting position and follow the players' moves as you read.

White	Black
1. e2 – e4	e7 – e6

Although White begins by boldly advancing his e-pawn two squares, Black is more restrained and moves her e-pawn only one square.

| 2. d2 – d4 | d7 – d5 |

This time both players move their other central pawn (the d-pawn) two squares forward. You can see that White now has the option of capturing Black's pawn on d5, using the white pawn on e4. If White leaves his pawn on e4, it may be captured by Black's pawn on d5.

In his next move, the third of the game, White chooses a different strategy.

3. e4 – e5

Instead of capturing on d5, White has decided to try setting up a strong pawn formation on d4 and e5.

3. ...   c7 – c5

Black responds with an attack at the base of White's **pawn chain**. By moving her pawn to c5, Black is now ready to capture the white pawn on d4.

4. c2 – c3

White moves to defend the base of his pawn chain. If Black now captures on d4 (4. . . . c5 × d4), White can recapture with his c-pawn (5. c3 × d4.), keeping his central pawn chain intact. Alternatively, Black can leave the pawn on c5 or play . . . c5–c4.

◄ **The position after** White's fourth move in the game described above. Note that the black pawn on d5 cannot advance to d4 because it is blocked by White's pawn, and the black pawn on e6 cannot advance to e5. Similarly, White's pawn on d4 is unable to advance to d5, and his e-pawn cannot move to e6.

En passant captures

The **en passant** capture is a special option that applies if a pawn moves from its 2nd **rank** to its 4th in one turn. It can then be captured by an enemy pawn positioned on an adjacent file, as though it had advanced only to its 3rd rank.

Looking at the chessboard below will clarify this. White has just moved his e-pawn from e2 to e4. If White had advanced his pawn only one square, to e3, Black would have been able to capture it with her pawn on d4. By advancing his e-pawn to e4 in one move, White hopes to sneak past the black pawn on d4. However, the en passant rule allows Black to capture White's e-pawn and move to e3, just as if White had played e2 to e3 in his previous move.

The en passant rule was introduced only a few centuries ago. Originally, pawns could advance only one square at a time, even on their first move. When the rules of chess were changed to speed up the game, players realized that a pawn might be able to take "unfair" advantage of the double-pawn move to evade capture. That is why the en passant rule was devised.

An en passant capture may only be made immediately after the double-pawn advance. The captured pawn must always have just moved from its 2nd to its 4th rank, while the pawn making the capture must always be on the rank next to the pawn that has moved, as in the example given below.

Remember that in **algebraic notation**, an en passant capture is recorded as ep—for example, . . . d4 × e3 ep.

▶ **On this chessboard,** White's last move was to advance his pawn from e2 to e4. Because of the en passant rule, Black can take advantage of this double-pawn advance and capture White's e-pawn by moving her own d-pawn diagonally to e3.

Pawn promotion

Although pawns are weak pieces, they are very important to the outcome of a game. If a pawn reaches its 8th **rank** — for White's pawns, this is the 8th rank on the board, and for Black's pawns, the 1st rank — it is promoted immediately, to become a queen, rook, bishop, or knight — whatever the player who owns it chooses to make it. A pawn that reaches its 8th rank must be promoted in this way, but it cannot become a king.

Players are allowed to promote more than one pawn. They can make all their pawns queens, if they wish, even if their original queen is still on the board. Alternatively, they can make eight new knights, bishops, or rooks, or any combination of the four pieces that adds up to eight.

Because the queen is the most powerful piece on the board, players who promote a pawn usually choose to make it a queen. An example of a game in which a player promotes a pawn to a queen is given on the chessboard below and at the top of the facing page. But, despite the usefulness of the queen, there are some rare cases when it is better to choose a different piece to promote (see game 1 on pages 58–59).

There are two ways of recording a pawn's promotion in **algebraic notation**. The piece that is chosen can be indicated by putting its letter in brackets, for example, c7–c8(Q). Another way is to use an = (equals) sign, for example, c7–c8 = Q.

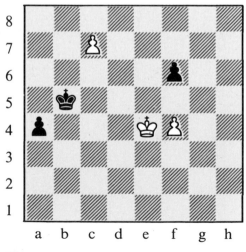

◄ **When a pawn** reaches its 8th rank it must be promoted to another piece. With the pieces in the position shown here, the players' chances appear to be roughly equal — each of them has two pawns and a king. But it is White's turn to move and one of his pawns has reached its 7th rank.

► **Compare this board** with the one at the bottom of the facing page and you'll see that White decided to advance his pawn from c7 to c8, making it into a queen. This promotion has given White a big advantage, as Black doesn't have a queen.

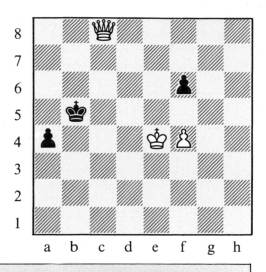

Review quiz 2

Set up your chessboard in the starting position and play through the following sequence of moves.

	White	Black
1.	e2 – e4	e7 – e6
2.	d2 – d4	d7 – d5
3.	e4 – e5	c7 – c5
4.	c2 – c3	Nb8 – c6
5.	Ng1 – f3	f7 – f5

Your chessboard should now look like the one above right. It is White's move next. Using full algebraic notation, list all the pawn moves that White is able to make, including those that would result in a capture.

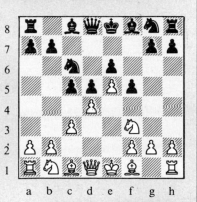

Start with the pawn on a2 and work your way across the board to the pawn on h2.

Answers on page 35

The Knight

The knight is one of the **minor pieces** in the chess set. The other is the bishop. They are roughly equal in strength and each of them is worth approximately three pawns (see "Values of the Pieces," page 45). Both the knight and the bishop are less powerful, and therefore less valuable, than rooks and queens.

The knight's move is L-shaped and can be made in any direction. It can travel two squares vertically, then one square horizontally, or two squares horizontally, then one square vertically. Alternatively, it can move one square horizontally, then two squares vertically, or one square vertically, then two squares horizontally.

The knight is the only chess piece that can jump over other pieces on the board, as the diagram below illustrates. (It may help to think of the knight as a horse leaping over fences.) The knight captures in exactly the same way that it moves, replacing the chess piece that occupies the square it lands on.

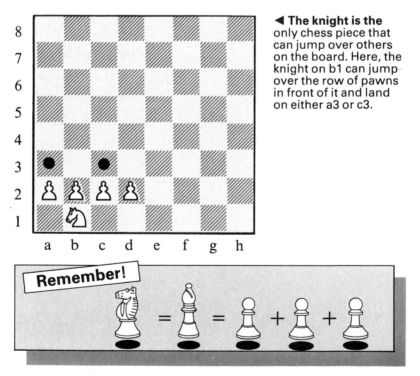

◀ **The knight is the** only chess piece that can jump over others on the board. Here, the knight on b1 can jump over the row of pawns in front of it and land on either a3 or c3.

34

◀ ▲ The knight's move is
L-shaped and can be made in
any direction. These are some of
the moves available to it.

Looking at the diagram below will give you some idea of the range of moves open to the knight — try them out for yourself, using your chessboard and pieces.

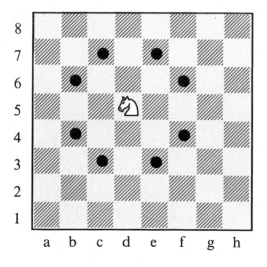

◀ **From d5 in the** middle of an empty board, the knight has eight moves available to it — to c7, e7, f6, f4, e3, c3, b4, or b6.

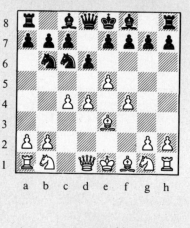

Review quiz 3

Place your chess pieces in the starting position and play through the following sequence of moves.

	White	Black
1.	e2 – e4	Ng8 – f6
2.	e4 – e5	Nf6 – d5
3.	c2 – c4	Nd5 – b6
4.	d2 – d4	d7 – d6
5.	f2 – f4	Nb8 – c6
6.	Bc1 – e3	

Your pieces should be in the position shown on the board right. Now list all the knight moves that Black can make.

Answers on page 39

The Bishop

The bishop moves diagonally and can travel any number of squares along one diagonal each move until blocked by another piece.

Players begin the game with two bishops, one on a light-colored square and the other on a dark-colored square. Because they move diagonally, bishops are restricted to the color square they start on and are therefore weaker pieces than rooks or queens, which can move horizontally and vertically.

► ▼ The bishop's move is diagonal and is always on the same color squares as it starts on. It can travel any number of squares until blocked by an occupied square.

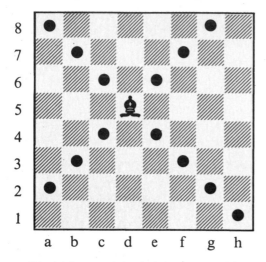

◄ **From d5 in the**
middle of an empty
board, the bishop can
move to 13 different
squares — c6, b7, a8,
e6, f7, g8, e4, f3, g2,
h1, c4, b3, or a2.

The bishop and the knight are roughly equal in strength, but there are times when one is more useful than the other. In **open positions**, with clear diagonals that offer the bishop freedom of movement, the bishop is the stronger of the two. But in **closed positions**, when there are chains of pieces along the diagonals, the bishop has difficulty moving around the board quickly because it cannot travel past an occupied square. In these cases the knight is more useful, because it can jump over other pieces. (Remember the analogy of the knight as a horse leaping obstacles.)

◄ **The bishop**
captures in the same
way that it moves.
Here, the white bishop
on g2 can capture the
black knight on c6 or
the black bishop on
the h3 square.

38

Answers to review quiz 3

... Nb6 – a4   ... Nb6 – d7   ... Nc6 × d4
... Nb6 × c4   ... Nc6 – a5   ... Nc6 × e5
... Nb6 – d5   ... Nc6 – b4   ... Nc6 – b8

Review quiz 4

Set up your chessboard and pieces in the starting position and play through the sequence of moves listed on the right.

	White	Black
1.	e2 – e4	Nb8 – c6
2.	Bf1 – b5	d7 – d6
3.	d2 – d3	Bc8 – d7
4.	Bb5 × c6	Bd7 × c6
5.	Nb1 – d2	f7 – f5
6.	e4 × f5	

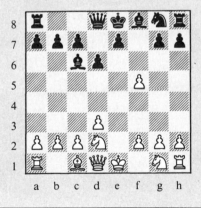

Your pieces should now be in the position shown left. List all the bishop moves that Black can make. Also list all the bishop moves White would be able to make if it were his turn to move.

Answers on page 42

39

The Rook

Rooks are stronger pieces than knights or bishops. A rook is usually worth roughly the same as a bishop and two pawns, or a knight and two pawns. Rooks and queens are the **major pieces**.

The rook can move any number of squares in a straight line along a **rank** or **file**, but in one direction only each turn. It captures in exactly the same way that it moves. When placed in the center of an empty board the rook has 14 **legal moves** available to it, as the diagram opposite shows.

Rooks are not allowed to jump over an occupied square, except in the special case of **castling** (see pages 48–49).

◄ ▼ Rooks travel in straight lines along ranks and files. They can move any number of squares in one turn, until blocked by an occupied square.

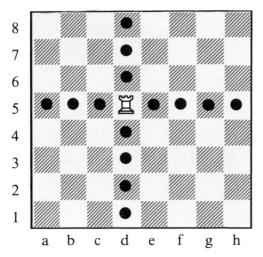

◄ **When placed on d5** in the middle of an empty board, the rook has 14 legal moves available to it.

▶ **Rooks capture in** the same way that they move. Here, the white rook on e7 can travel to e8, e6, d7, or c7, and it can capture the black pawn on f7 or the black queen on b7. It cannot move to e5 because that square is occupied by one of its own pawns.

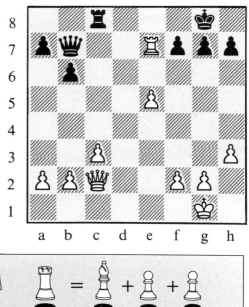

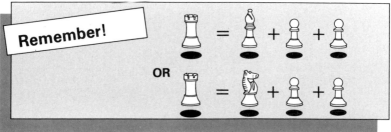

Remember!

41

From the starting position, play through the following sequence of moves.

	White	Black
1.	d2 – d4	h7 – h5
2.	c2 – c4	Rh8 – h6
3.	Bc1 × h6	Ng8 × h6
4.	Nb1 – c3	c7 – c5
5.	Ra1 – c1	c5 × d4
6.	Ng1 – f3	d4 × c3

Your board should now look like the one below. List all the rook moves that White can make from this position.

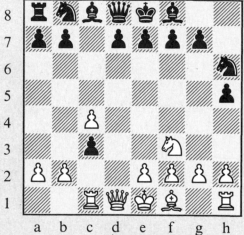

Answers on page 44

Black's bishop moves:
. . . Bc6 – b5
. . . Bc6 – a4
. . . Bc6 – d7
. . . Bc6 – d5
. . . Bc6 – e4
. . . Bc6 – f3
. . . Bc6 × g2

White's bishop moves:
White can't make any bishop moves with the board in this position because his bishop on c1 is blocked by his knight on d2 and pawn on b2 — bishops cannot jump over pieces.

The Queen

The queen is the most powerful piece in the chess set, because it can move any number of squares and in eight different directions — forward, backward, to either side, and along all diagonals. The queen combines the moves of the rook and the bishop, and if placed on d5 in the middle of an empty board, it can attack or travel to 27 different squares. But queens cannot jump over occupied squares — only knights can do this.

▶ ▼ The queen can move in any direction — along ranks, files, and diagonals — any number of squares, until blocked by an occupied square.

Because it is so powerful, the queen is the piece most often chosen for **promotion** when a pawn reaches its 8th rank. (You may find it useful to look again at the description of pawn promotion on pages 32–33.)

The queen captures in the same way that it moves. In the position illustrated on the board at the bottom of this page, the white queen on h6 can capture the black pawns on g6 or h7, or the black bishop on g7. It cannot move to h2 because that square is occupied by a white pawn, but it can retreat along the diagonal to c1.

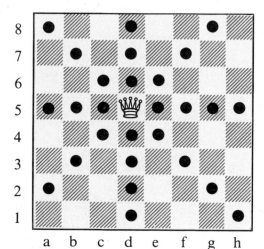

◄ **From d5 in the** middle of an empty board, the queen can attack or travel to 27 different squares.

▼ **Here, the white** queen on h6 can capture on g6, h7, or g7. The black queen is almost hemmed in by its own color pieces and can travel only to b8, c8, or e7.

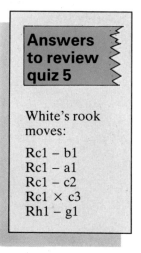
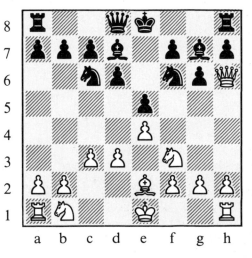

Set your chessboard up in the starting position and play
through the following sequence of moves:

	White	Black
1.	c2 – c4	e7 – e5
2.	Nb1 – c3	Bf8 – b4
3.	Qd1 – b3	Bb4 × c3
4.	Qb3 × c3	Qd8 – g5
5.	d2 – d3	

Your pieces should now be
in the position shown right.
List all the queen moves
that Black can make.

Answers on page 47

Values of the Pieces

In the chess set, the queen and the rook are the **major pieces** because
they are the most powerful pieces on the board, while the less
valuable bishops and knights are the **minor pieces**.

An approximate value can be given to each piece apart from the
king. If a pawn is counted as one unit of strength, then a queen is
worth nine pawns, a rook is worth five, and bishops and knights are
worth three pawns each. This is a very rough guide, however, and in
certain cases the value of a piece can dramatically increase or
decrease, according to what it can achieve. Together, for example, a
bishop and a knight are more useful than a rook and pawn combination, even though the value of each pair is six pawns.

These rough values can help you decide when you should or
shouldn't **capture** your opponent's pieces, and whether you should
worry about your own pieces being captured. The values can also
help in assessing which side is ahead. With careful play the side with
the highest total piece value, or the most **material**, will usually (but
not always) win the game.

The King

Although the queen is the most powerful chess piece, the king is the most important and must be guarded very carefully at all times. If your king is threatened with **checkmate**, or certain capture, the game is over and you have lost. This is why the king cannot be valued — it doesn't matter how many other pieces you have if you are going to lose your king.

Normally, the king can travel in any direction one square at a time, capturing in the same way. But once during a game the king can make a special move called **castling**. This move involves the rook as well and it is described on pages 48–49.

◀ ▼ The king can move in all directions but, unless castling, it must travel just one square at a time.

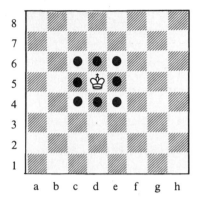

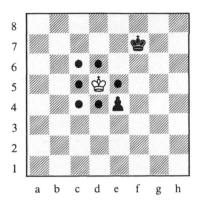

The chessboards above show how the king moves. On the one on the left, the white king on d5 can make a total of eight **legal moves**, to any of the squares marked by a dot.

On the board above right the white king is again on d5, but this time it can move to only seven squares — c6, c5, c4, d6, d4, e5, or e4 (this last move captures the black pawn). The white king cannot advance to e6 because the black king on f7 is attacking that square and it is **illegal** to make a move that places your king in **check**. (If it were Black's turn to move, her king could not advance to e6 for the same reason.)

Remember

It is illegal to make a move that places your king in check.

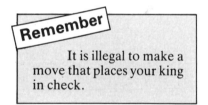

Answers to review quiz 6

. . . Qg5 – h5	. . . Qg5 × g2	. . . Qg5 – h6
. . . Qg5 – f5	. . . Qg5 – h4	. . . Qg5 – f4
. . . Qg5 – g6	. . . Qg5 – f6	. . . Qg5 – e3
. . . Qg5 – g4	. . . Qg5 – e7	. . . Qg5 – d2+
. . . Qg5 – g3	. . . Qg5 – d8	. . . Qg5 × c1+

Did you remember to write the + (plus) signs to indicate check after the last two moves in this list?

Castling

Castling is the only time during a chess game that a player can move two pieces on the same turn. It is a special move that involves both the king and the rook, and it was invented during the 16th century as a way of speeding up the game.

The castling move can be made only if both pieces are still in their starting positions, as on the board below left. The king's path to its new square must not be blocked by another piece, and the rook's path must also be clear.

To castle, the king moves two squares toward the rook on its right or its left. That rook (now the one nearest to the·king) is then allowed to jump over the king and land on the square next to it, as shown on the board below right.

This move is the only time that the king can travel more than one square at a time, and each player is allowed to make the castling move just once during a game.

Castling is a useful way of protecting the king, as it moves nearer to the corner of the board where it is less vulnerable to attack from an enemy piece than it is on the central **files**. Castling also has the advantage of bringing the rook, which is an important attacking piece, into play.

Before castling

▲ **Players can make the castling** move only when their king and rook are still in their starting positions, as here.

After castling

▲ **White has castled by moving** his king to the right (king's side). Black has castled her king to the queen's side.

Players can castle to either side of the board and, in general, you should aim to castle early in the game. Castling on the **queen's side** (files **a** to **d**) is sometimes called "castling long," as there are more squares between the king and the rook on that side of the board and the rook jumps one extra square. Castling **king's side** (files **e** to **h**) is also called "castling short." Castling to the king's side is usually safer than castling queen's side, as it puts the king deeper into a corner of the board.

In chess notation king's side castling is written 0–0, while queen's side castling is written 0–0–0.

▶ **There is one** exception to the rule that prevents castling if it means moving a piece across an attacked square — the queen's rook (on a1 or a8) can do this. Here, the white bishop on g3 is attacking b8, but because the king does not pass over or land on b8 the castling move can take place.

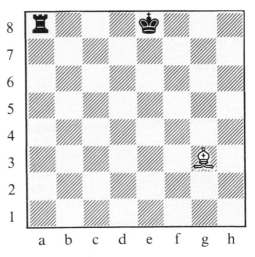

It is important to remember that players cannot castle if their king is in **check**, or if castling means moving their king or rook across or onto a square that is being attacked by an enemy piece. The one exception to this last rule is illustrated on the board above. When castling queen's side, the rook on a1 or a8 may move across an attacked square. In fact, the only squares this applies to are b1 for White and b8 for Black.

Finally, when castling, you should always move your king first. By moving your king two squares you are indicating very clearly that you intend to castle. If you were to move your rook first this would not be absolutely clear — you might be planning to place your rook next to your king and to leave your king where it is. If you do move your rook first in a serious game, your opponent could use the **touch-move rule** to insist that you are making a rook move, thereby preventing you from castling.

Here are some examples of castling for you to try out. Before writing down your answers to each question, check that the rules which prevent castling do not apply.

1. Begin by setting up your chessboard and pieces in the starting position. Then play through the following sequence of moves:

	White	Black
1.	d2 – d4	g7 – g6
2.	c2 – c4	Bf8 – g7
3.	Nb1 – c3	Ng8 – f6
4.	Bc1 – f4	Rh8 – f8
5.	Qd1 – d2	Rf8 – h8

Your chessboard should now look like the one above. It is White's turn to move — can he castle? If it were Black's turn, would she be able to castle?

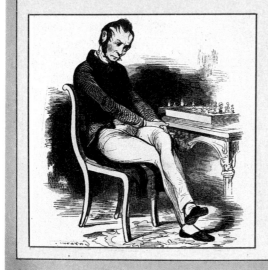

◄ **Allow yourself** plenty of time to concentrate on the game ahead when playing chess. How will your opponent respond to your move?

2. The games on the chessboards below are already underway. Look at the position of the pieces on each board very carefully before writing down your answers.

The answers to this quiz are all on page 52

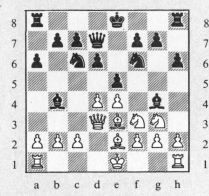

▲ (A) **White's turn to move**
Can he castle king's side?
Can he castle queen's side?

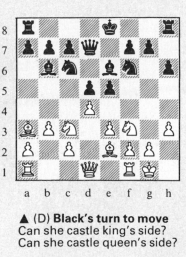

▲ (B) **Black's turn to move**
Can she castle king's side?
Can she castle queen's side?

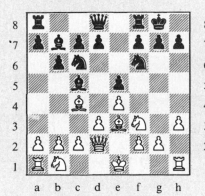

▲ (C) **White's turn to move**
Can he castle king's side?
Can he castle queen's side?

▲ (D) **Black's turn to move**
Can she castle king's side?
Can she castle queen's side?

1. In this first game White could castle queen's side by moving his king to c1 and his rook from a1 to d1.

If it were Black's turn to move, she wouldn't be able to castle king's side because she has already moved the rook on h8 – to f8 and then back to h8. Even though this rook is now on its original square, it has been moved from its starting position and Black cannot use it to castle king's side. Black may be able to castle queen's side at a later stage in the game, but at present the squares between her king and the rook on a8 are blocked by her knight, bishop, and queen.

2. (A) White cannot castle king's side or queen's side because his king is in check from the black bishop on b4. You cannot castle out of check.

2. (B) Black cannot castle king's side because the square g8 to which her king would move is being attacked by the white knight on h6. If Black were to castle king's side, her king would be placed in check and it is illegal to make a move that places your king in check.

But Black can castle queen's side, as although the white knight on a6 is attacking the square b8, the black king will not be on b8 after castling and will not cross b8 during the castling move. (Remember that when castling queen's side, the rook is allowed to cross an attacked square.)

2. (C) White can castle king's side but not queen's side, as his knight on b1 is blocking the path of his rook on a1. For castling to be possible, all the squares between the king and the rook must be empty.

2. (D) Black can castle queen's side but not king's side, as the white bishop on a3 is attacking the f8 square, which Black's king would cross during castling.

Check

Check is a move that threatens an opponent's king with **capture**. Since losing it means the end of the game, the king must be saved immediately.

On the first board below, White's king on g1 is in check from Black's bishop on c5, but there are three ways of saving it. The first is to move the white king out of check.

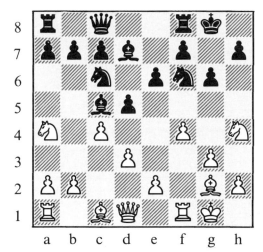

◀ **Here, White's king** on g1 is being attacked by Black's bishop on c5. The white king is in check and unless White saves it the game will be over — a win to Black.

▶ **One way White can** save his king is to move it out of check. Here, White has played Kg1–h1, removing his king from danger — on h1 the white king is no longer under attack.

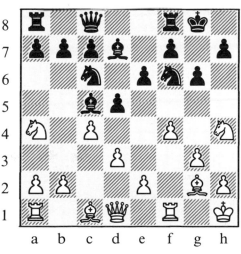

The bottom board on the previous page illustrates how White can play Kg1–h1 to move his king out of check. White's second option is to capture the piece that is attacking his king — in this game, Black's bishop on c5 (see the board below).

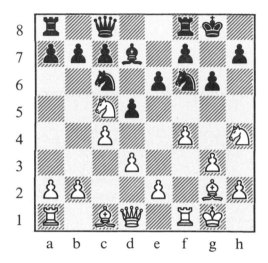

◄ **White can also save** his king by capturing the attacking piece. Here, White has played Na4–c5, using his knight to take the black bishop.

► **Another way that** White can save his king is to block Black's line of attack. Here, White has played e2–e3, placing his pawn between the black bishop and his king on g1.

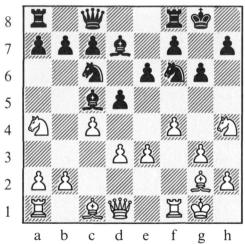

White's final option is to place one of his other pieces between his king and Black's bishop, thereby blocking the black bishop's line of attack. In this game, there are four ways White can do this and the board above shows one.

Another way that White could block the black bishop's attack would be to advance his d-pawn from d3 to d4. Alternatively, White could move his bishop, playing Bc1–e3, or he could place his rook between his king and the black bishop, playing Rf1–f2.

Bear in mind that the king may never be moved to a square where it would be in check. On the board below White cannot move his king to d1, because that square is being attacked by Black's queen on the d8 square.

Players are also not allowed to make a move that would open their king to check. On the board below White cannot move his knight from c3, because moving the knight would leave open a clear path of attack along the diagonal for Black's bishop on a5.

▶ **Players are not** allowed to move their king to a square where it would be in check, or to make a move that would open their king to check. Here, White cannot play Ke1–d1 or move his knight from the c3 square.

▼ **This delicate 14th** century miniature depicts a game of chess between an Indian envoy and a noble of the Persian court of Khusran I.

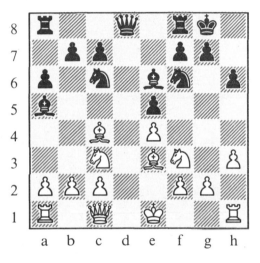

Checkmate

Checkmate is when the king is in **check** and cannot escape, and it is the object of every chess game. If your opponent cannot move or defend the king, the game is over and you have won. Here are four examples of checkmating positions.

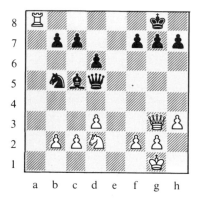

On the board above, Black's king on g8 is in check from the white rook on a8. The only vacant squares to which the black king can move are f8 and h8 (remember, the king moves one square at a time), but if it moves to one of these squares, the white rook on a8 will still be able to capture it. Black cannot escape from the check by moving her king.

Nor can Black interpose any piece between her king and the white rook. If Black could move one of her pieces to b8, c8, d8, e8, or f8, the check would be blocked.

Finally, Black cannot capture the white rook as none of her pieces are attacking it. Black has been checkmated.

Here we see a drastic example of a boxed-in king. The black knight on h3 has the white king in check on the board above. Because knights can jump over other pieces, you can never get out of a knight check by moving a piece between the knight and the king. White cannot block this check, nor can he capture the black knight — none of his pieces are attacking it.

White would like to move his king out of the check, but the only vacant squares next to it are g2 and h1, and both of these squares are being attacked by the black bishop on f3. None of the three ways of saving a king is available to White. His king has been checkmated and Black has won the game.

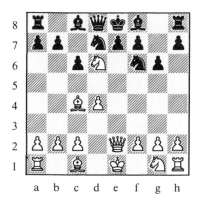

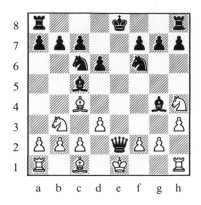

This next example has happened a few times in games between experienced players. Set up your chessboard and play through the following sequence of moves:

	White	Black
1.	e2 – e4	c7 – c6
2.	d2 – d4	d7 – d5
3.	Nb1 – c3	d5 × e4
4.	Nc3 × e4	Nb8 – d7
5.	Bf1 – c4	Ng8 – f6
6.	Qd1 – e2	g7 – g6
7.	Ne4 – d6 checkmate	

On the board above, you can see that the black king is in check from the white knight on d6. It looks as though Black can capture this knight with her pawn on e7. But removing this pawn from e7 would leave Black's king in check from the white queen on e2. Because you cannot make a move that places your king in check, the move . . . e7 × d6 is **illegal**.

Black cannot capture White's knight, and all the squares next to her king are occupied.

On the board above, the white king on e1 is being checkmated by the black queen on e2. The black queen is defended by the bishop on g4. White cannot capture the black queen (Ke1 × e2), because that would leave his king on a square that is being attacked by the black bishop.

Because the other squares adjacent to White's king (d1, f1, and d2) are all under attack from the black queen, White cannot move his king anywhere. Black has won the game.

Short games won by checkmate

Here are a few more examples of games won very quickly by **checkmate**. It is extremely unusual for a strong player to be checkmated early in the game as in the examples given here, but it does happen sometimes.

Game 1

Set up your chessboard in the starting position and play through the following sequence of moves:

White	Black
1. e2 – e4	e7 – e5
2. f2 – f4	e5 × f4
3. b2 – b3	Qd8 – h4+
4. g2 – g3	f4 × g3
5. h2 – h3	g3 – g2+

This last move is **check**, even though the black pawn making the move is not attacking the white king. As the board below shows, by moving her pawn from g3 to g2 Black has opened up a line of attack to the white king for the black queen on h4. The black queen is giving check in the fifth move. This type of check is called **discovered check**.

6. Ke1 – e2	Qh4 × e4+
7. Ke2 – f2	g2 × h1 = N
	checkmate

Black has given check by advancing her pawn to its 8th rank and **underpromoting** it to a knight (see pages 32–33). Black could have made this pawn into a queen, but although a queen is much more valuable than a

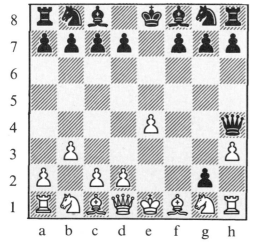

◄ **Discovered check is** when one piece is moved out of the path of another, enabling the second piece to give check. Black has just played . . . g3–g2, opening the white king to check from her queen on h4.

knight, in certain cases a knight is more useful.

Because knights can jump over other pieces, White cannot escape this check by moving a piece between the promoted black pawn and his king. Nor can White move his king, as the vacant squares next to it are being attacked by Black's queen on e4. Black has won the game.

If Black had made her h-pawn into a queen, playing . . . g2 ×h1=Q, she would probably have won the game eventually because this would have given her two queens to White's one.

Game 2

Again from the starting position, play through the following sequence of moves. The chessboard below shows the position after Black's 14th move.

	White	Black
1.	e2 – e4	e7 – e6
2.	d2 – d4	d7 – d5
3.	e4 – e5	c7 – c5
4.	c2 – c3	c5 × d4
5.	c3 × d4	Bf8 – b4+
6.	Nb1 – c3	Nb8 – c6
7.	Ng1 – f3	Ng8 – e7
8.	Bf1 – d3	0–0

Black **castles** king's side (see pages 48–49).

9.	Bd3 × h7+	Kg8 × h7
10.	Nf3 – g5+	Kh7 – g6
11.	h2 – h4	Nc6 × d4
12.	Qd1 – g4	f7 – f5
13.	h4 – h5+	Kg6 – h6
14.	Ng5 × e6+	g7 – g5
15.	h5 × g6 ep checkmate	

White captures the black g5 pawn **en passant**. Removing the black pawn from g5 opens the line of attack for White's bishop on c1 and rook on h1.

► **The position after** Black's 14th move in the game described above. White is about to play h5 × g6, taking Black's pawn on g5 en passant and checkmating her king.

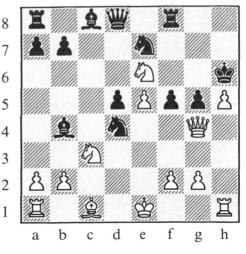

Black cannot escape the check by capturing the pawn on g6 or by moving her king to g5 or h5, as these squares are being attacked by the white queen on g4. The black king cannot move to h7 as here it would be in check from White's g6 pawn and h1 rook, while on g7 it would be in check from his knight on e6.

Game 3

The next game was played in 1858. In those days it was common for very strong players to give their opponents **odds**, by allowing them some advantage in pieces at the start of the game.

In this game White was Paul Morphy, the strongest player of his day. Morphy gave the odds of his queen's rook, so remove the white rook from a1 before you start playing the moves.

White	Black
1. e2 – e4	e7 – e5
2. Ng1 – f3	Nb8 – c6
3. Bf1 – c4	Ng8 – f6
4. Nf3 – g5	d7 – d5
5. e4 × d5	Nf6 × d5
6. Ng5 × f7	Ke8 × f7
7. Qd1 – f3 +	Kf7 – e6
8. Nb1 – c3	Nc6 – d4
9. Bc4 × d5 +	Ke6 – d6
10. Qf3 – f7	Bc8 – e6
11. Bd5 × e6	Nd4 × e6
12. Nc3 – e4 +	Kd6 – d5
13. c2 – c4 +	Kd5 × e4
14. Qf7 × e6	Qd8 – d4
15. Qe6 – g4 +	Ke4 – d3
16. Qg4 – e2 +	Kd3 – c2
17. d2 – d3 +	Kc2 × c1
18. 0–0 checkmate	

By **castling** king's side, Morphy places the black king in check to his rook on f1. Black cannot escape the check, so Morphy wins the game.

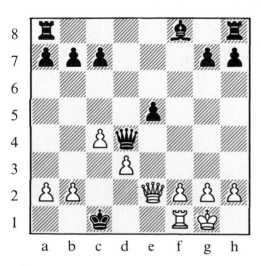

◀ **Black's king is in** check to the white rook on f1. Black cannot move her king to escape the check — on c2 and d2 it would be attacked by the white queen, which also defends the pawn on b2. Black has been checkmated and White has won.

Stalemate

Stalemate is when the player whose turn it is to move cannot make any **legal moves** but is *not* in **check**. It ends the game immediately, as a draw, and it usually occurs when there are very few pieces left on the board.

In competition chess, a win counts as one point while a draw is only half a point. A loss scores zero.

► **Black's king is in** stalemate here. It has no legal moves available to it, as all the squares next to it are being attacked by White's pawn and king.

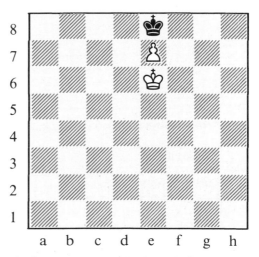

On the board above it is Black's turn to move. Her king on e8 cannot make any legal moves because all of the squares next to it are being attacked by one or both of White's pieces. The squares d8 and f8 are both under attack from the white pawn on e7, while the squares d7, e7, and f7 are all being attacked by the white king. This game has therefore ended in stalemate and the result is a draw.

It is useful to discover just how near to victory a stalemate can be. If it were White's turn to move on the board above, and not Black's, the game would be an easy win for White.

To see how White would win the game, set your chessboard up in the position shown above and play through these moves:

	White	Black
1.	Ke6 – f6	Ke8 – d7
2.	Kf6 – f7!	

By playing Ke6–f6 in the first move, White allows Black one legal move: Ke8–d7. The black king cannot move anywhere else, as all the other squares next to it are still under attack from the white pawn and king.

White's second move, Kf6–f7, gives his pawn the protection of his king — for Black to take the white pawn on e7 is illegal as it would be moving her king into check. At the same time, White's move makes it impossible for the black king to return to e8, since that square is now under attack from the white king on f7.

Black must move her king elsewhere, but nothing she does will help her. The path is open for White to advance his pawn on e7 to its 8th rank and **promote** it to a queen (e7–e8 = Q). White can then win by using his king and queen against Black's **lone king** (see page 123).

Another example of the care needed near the end of a game can be seen by comparing the positions illustrated below and on the opposite page. White is one queen up and can win the game on his next move.

With the pieces in the position shown below, White can deliver **checkmate** by playing Qb3–b7. The black king will be in check to the white queen, with no safe square to move to. But what if White moves his queen only as far as b6?

With the white queen on b6, as on the board opposite, Black still doesn't have any legal moves open to her. But this time Black's king is not in check. The game therefore ends in a draw by stalemate and White earns just half a point.

It is easier to make this kind of mistake than you might think. In a rapid game tournament in Canada in 1988, I saw World Champion Gary Kasparov allow a draw by stalemate when he was a queen ahead.

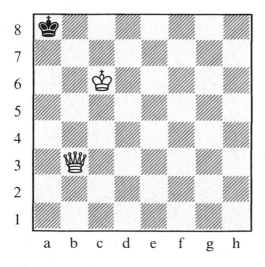

◀ **In this position** White can deliver checkmate by advancing his queen to b7.

► **This position is** stalemate. Black's king cannot move, but it isn't in check.

▼ **A game of chess** reaches its last tense moves. The opponents in this game are Italians of the late 16th century.

4: The Opening

This is the first phase of the game, during which the players bring out their pieces ready for the battle ahead. There are many well-known chess openings, which can be learned by heart, but as a beginner it is better to start by understanding the strategies that underlie them. Some of the best-known openings are discussed on pages 69–89.

First Principles

Some basic principles of opening theory follow on pages 65–68. Study them carefully and attempt to put them into practice when you begin playing. Don't try to bend these principles until you understand them thoroughly.

There are also some general maxims of play that are worth remembering, both in the opening and throughout the rest of the game. The most vital of these is:

- Don't blunder away material.

This type of mistake is the single most common cause of losing a game of chess. So, before making a move, ask yourself these two key questions:

- Is my opponent posing a threat that I've failed to recognize?

In other words, is your opponent attacking one or more of your pieces and, in doing so,

forcing you to take immediate defensive action?

- Does my intended move allow one of my own pieces to be taken or put **en prise**?

That is, will your piece be taken without compensation — are you planning to place it on a square where it is attacked but not defended, or where it may be captured by a piece less valuable than itself?

Asking yourself these questions before making a move will save you a number of games, while this final question will sometimes gain a useful opportunity:

- Has my opponent's last move given me the chance to take one or more enemy pieces safely?

Taking advantage of your opponent's mistakes is just as important as avoiding mistakes of your own.

Opening Strategy

1: Gain control of the center

The main purpose of the opening is to develop your chess pieces for the attack ahead. **Development** is the process of bringing out your pieces to squares where they are performing some useful function, and at this stage of a game, attacking the central squares is one of the most useful things a piece can do. As you move your pieces out toward your opponent's side of the chessboard, you will gradually gain control over more and more territory.

Control of the central squares of the board can be very important. It is a basic principle of military strategy to control high ground, and on the chessboard, that is the center. Pieces positioned in the center are very flexible and can switch their attack from one side of the board, or flank, to the other. Pieces at the edge of the board, on the other hand, have fewer moves available and cannot move easily to attack or defend the opposite flank.

▶ **The d4, d5, e4, and** e5 squares are the center of the chessboard. Try to place your d- and e-pawns on these squares early in the game.

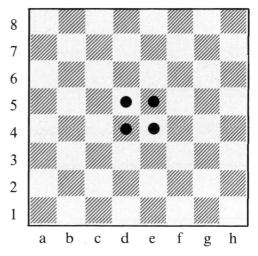

The center of a chessboard consists of the d4, d5, e4, and e5 squares, as the above diagram shows. It is sensible to try to place your d-pawn and e-pawn on these squares as early as possible in the game, and to support them with other pawns and pieces. An alternative to this type of direct occupation is to gain control of the center by aiming the attention of your pieces at these four vital squares (see page 76, Nimzo-Indian defense).

2: Look at ranks and diagonals

Other useful developing moves are those that put pressure along vital ranks and diagonals. One good example of this is **fianchetto**, a maneuver in which a knight's pawn (the b-pawn or the g-pawn) is advanced one square and the bishop developed behind it (to either b2 or g2 for White, or b7 or g7 for Black). The value of the move is that it mobilizes the bishop to gain control of the long diagonal (h1–a8 or a1–h8).

On the board below, for instance, once the knight on f3 moves, the bishop on g2 can attack along the h1–a8 diagonal. White has **castled** king's side and his king is safely tucked in behind an array of pawns and other pieces. This is a typical pattern of development for White and Black in many openings.

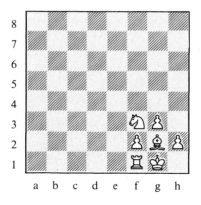

◀ The fianchettoed bishop.
White has advanced his g-pawn (g2–g3), enabling his bishop to move from f1 to g2 and thereby gaining control of the h1–a8 long diagonal.

3: Don't move the same piece twice in the opening

It is usually fruitless to move the same piece twice, because each chess piece controls or attacks a limited number of squares. A better strategy is to move several pieces out toward the center of the board, thereby allowing your chess army to work in harmony to control the greatest area.

4: Don't bring out your queen too soon

It is rarely a good idea to move the queen out during the opening. If the queen is advanced it is usually only one rank, so that it isn't too exposed. You may be tempted to use your queen to attack the enemy king or another of your opponent's pieces, but the response will probably be an attack on your queen, which will then be forced to retreat to safety. Bringing your queen into play too early can waste valuable moves. (There are, of course, exceptions to this rule — see pages 58 and 68.)

5: Try to make moves that achieve multiple goals

It is particularly useful to attack your opponent's pieces when developing your own. Instead of developing his or her own resources, your opponent will be forced to defend or move the attacked piece, thereby wasting a move (or **tempo**). A simple example of this strategy can be seen in the Center Counter game, which follows, an opening rarely played in master chess because it wastes valuable time.

The board below shows the position of the pieces after White's third move.

1. e2 – e4   d7 – d5
2. e4 × d5   Qd8 × d5
3. Nb1 – c3

The black queen on d5 is now being attacked by the white knight on c3. Black's next move must be to remove her queen from this attack. This will allow White to use his fourth move to develop another minor piece — by playing Bf1–c4 or Ng1–f3, for instance. White will then have two of his chess pieces in play, whereas Black, forced on the defensive, will have moved only her queen.

▶ **The position after White's** third move in the Center Counter game. Black's queen is being attacked by White's knight on c3. She will waste time removing her queen from this attack.

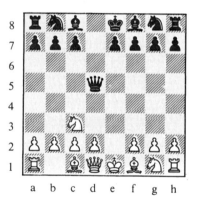

6: Don't delay the castling move

If you intend to **castle**, it is best to do so fairly early in the game, as the opportunity may be lost if you wait too long. Remember that you cannot castle once you have moved your king, while moving a rook means that you cannot castle to its side.

However, castling is usually not so important if you and your opponent have **exchanged** queens early in the game and neither of you has a queen on the board. The queen is the most important attacking piece, and if you've captured the enemy queen you will have less to fear from leaving your king on one of the central files.

7: Avoid moving your f-pawn too early

The f-pawn can be the source of major problems. At the start of the game it is positioned on a very weak square — f2 for White and f7 for Black — where it is only defended by the king (because of the way they move, neither the bishop nor the knight can protect it). But advancing your f-pawn too soon can create a permanent and crippling weakness in the squares near your king.

◀ **White's f-pawn** advance has left his king exposed to attack from either Black's bishop (. . . Bf8–c5 and . . . Bc5–f2 +) or her queen (. . . Qd8–h4 +).

An example of this is the King's Gambit, which was one of the most popular openings of the 19th century. The first moves of the King's Gambit are 1. e2–e4 e7–e5 and 2. f2–f4. The board above illustrates the position of the chess pieces after White's second move in this opening.

The King's Gambit has almost disappeared from major tournaments, because players have discovered that it places the white king in a dangerous position very early in the game. It is Black's turn to move, for example, and she can use her bishop to take control of the a7–g1 diagonal, starting with the move . . . Bf8–c5. This would make it difficult for White to castle king's side, as the g1 square is now under attack from the black bishop.

Another possible disadvantage for White is that in some cases Black can safely play the move . . . Qd8–h4 +, thereby disrupting the white king and forcing it to move away from e1 to escape the check. (This, of course, is one of those cases when it is advisable to bring out a queen early in the game.)

See pages 84–86 for two further variations of this opening.

Extracts from some of the best-known variations of openings play follow in the remainder of this chapter. White's opening move, e2–e4, in the first of these, the Ruy Lopez, is the most popular in chess. With it White opens lines for his queen and his king's bishop, while staking a claim in the center of the board. The great American player Bobby Fischer opened with e2–e4 in almost all his important games as White.

Ruy Lopez

Lopez was a 16th-century Spanish priest who was a favorite at the court of King Philip II. In 1561 he published a book of chess openings and general advice, which included the suggestion that the board be placed so that the sun is in the opponent's eyes!

This opening comes from that book. Its strategy is for White to exert indirect pressure on the black e-pawn, while attempting to play the central pawn advance d2–d4.

Set up your board in the starting position and play through the moves of this opening as you read. The chessboard below shows the position after White's third move.

1.	e2 – e4	e7 – e5
2.	Ng1 – f3	Nb8 – c6
3.	Bf1 – b5	

In his first three moves, White develops his king's-side pieces,

▶ **The position after** White's third move in the Ruy Lopez opening. White has developed his king's-side pieces, leaving the way open to castle.

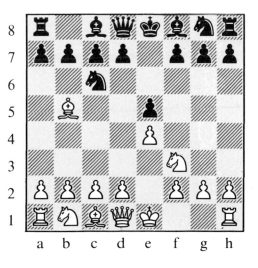

leaving the way open to castle. With his third move, White also puts pressure on Black's e-pawn by attacking the knight that defends it.

3. . . .   a7 – a6!

Black attacks White's bishop in order to drive it back.

At some point, Black will want to advance her d-pawn, but this will leave her knight on c6 **pinned** against her king on e8. (A pinned piece is one that is shielding a more valuable piece from attack; see also page 105.) Black won't be able to move her knight because this would place her king in **check** from the white bishop on b5, and it is **illegal** to make a move that places your king in check.

However, Black's third move should push the white bishop back to a4 to avoid capture by the black a-pawn. This will lessen the effect of the potential pin, and Black can attack the white bishop again later in the game.

White now removes his bishop from attack.

4. Bb5 – a4

An alternative fourth move for White is to capture the black knight at once, with Bb5×c6. This introduces the Exchange variation of the Ruy Lopez opening, and Black replies with 4. . . . d7×c6. After this it appears as though White can win a pawn by playing 5. Nf3

×e5, but Black's reply, 5. . . . Qd8–d4, attacks the white knight and the white e-pawn simultaneously. Since they cannot both be protected, White would lose the pawn advantage he gained on his fifth move (White had captured a knight and a pawn, while Black only had a bishop at that stage). That Black had brought out her queen in the opening would not matter, since in this case White cannot accomplish anything useful by attacking it.

But instead, Black now develops her king's knight and attacks the white e-pawn.

4. . . .   Ng8 – f6

Later, Black will want to play . . . b7–b5, attacking the white bishop again and destroying the potential pin on her knight. Experience has shown that it is foolish to play this move too early in the game.

5. 0–0

White **castles** king's side, protecting his king and preparing to occupy the center. If Black now takes the white e-pawn, with 5. . . . Nf6×e4, then White can respond by playing 6. Rf1–e1 or 6. Qd1–e2. This will force Black to do something about her attacked knight on e4, and White will regain the e-pawn.

5. . . .   Bf8 – e7

Black **develops** her king's bishop and blocks the e-file. She is now ready to castle king's side.

6. Rf1 – e1   b7 – b5

White defends his e-pawn. Black's move enables her to fend off the white bishop on a4 and avoid **pinning** her knight when she advances her d-pawn.

7. Ba4 – b3   d7 – d6

White removes his bishop from attack. Black opens the c8–h3 diagonal for her queen's bishop, at the same time supporting her pawn on e5 — if the white knight on f3 takes the black e-pawn, Black can capture the knight with . . . d6 × e5.

In this extract from Ruy Lopez, one of the most subtle yet most popular of openings, you will have noticed that White moved his bishop several times, apparently wasting moves, or **tempi**. In this case, however, White's moves were in response to Black's threats and so the moves were justified.

Sicilian Defense — Dragon Variation

The Sicilian defense is the most popular of all chess openings. Indeed, more than a quarter of all master games are Sicilians. The continuing popularity of this opening lies in the possibilities it gives to Black for pursuing an active fight.

Black has two main aims in the Sicilian defense. Firstly, she tries to attack White's e-pawn, usually by positioning her king's knight on f6, and sometimes with her queen's bishop on b7 as well. Secondly, Black sets up an attack along the c-file by developing her queen's rook to c8.

An extract from this defense follows. From the starting position, play through the moves as you read.

1. e2 – e4   c7 – c5

Black attacks the center from the c-file, thus creating an unbalanced pawn structure. This usually leads to sharp positions

that offer interesting possibilities for both sides.

2. Ng1 – f3   d7 – d6

Black opens the c8–h3 diagonal for her queen's bishop, at the same time preventing White from advancing his pawn safely to e5. (At e5, White's pawn could now be taken by the black d-pawn.) This is the most popular second move of this defense, and a favorite of the American, Bobby Fischer.

3. d2 – d4   c5 × d4
4. Nf3 × d4   Ng8 – f6

Black achieves her first aim — her knight on f6 is attacking the

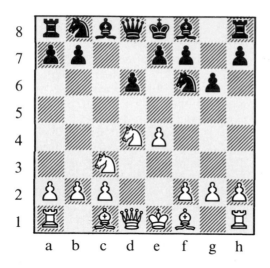

◄ **The position after**
Black's seventh move in the Dragon variation of the Sicilian defense. Black's pawn structure at this stage is said to look like the outline of a dragon.

white e-pawn. White now moves to defend his pawn.

| 5. | Nb1 – c3 | g7 – g6 |

Black's last move introduces the Dragon variation of the Sicilian defense. The name derives from Black's pawn structure, which is said to resemble the outline of a dragon. (The position of the pieces at this stage is shown on the board above.)

Black's next move is to advance her king's bishop to g7, where it puts pressure on the long diagonal (a1–h8). She is also preparing to **castle**.

| 6. | Bc1 – e3 | Bf8 – g7 |
| 7. | Bf1 – e2 | Nb8 – c6 |

White and Black are making normal developing moves, and it would be logical for both of them to castle king's side on their next moves to give their kings greater safety.

Black hopes eventually to play the move . . . d6–d5, which will give her pieces greater freedom of action.

French Defense — Classical Variation

Although the Sicilian produces dynamic games, the French defense often resembles siege warfare. It is a very solid defense to the opening White move e2–e4. White positions his pawns at d4 and e5, while Black blocks them with pawns at d5 and e6. The center of the board is then closed by these two conflicting **pawn chains** (see the board on the facing page).

From the starting position, play through the moves as you read.

1. e2 – e4   e7 – e6

Black accepts an inferior position in the center, in return for the safety provided by her pawn chain. She has shut in her queen's bishop on c8, and part of her strategy will be concerned with either freeing this piece or **exchanging** it for another piece of equal value. A **bad bishop** (one that's trapped behind its own pawns, which are on squares the same color as itself — see also page 102) is worth far less than an actively positioned knight.

2. d2 – d4

In his first two moves White establishes a hold on the center by placing two mobile pawns in the middle of the board. He also creates space behind the pawns for his pieces to develop.

2. . . .   d7 – d5

A mobile **pawn center** is a powerful tool for attack, thus Black blocks the white pawns.

3. Nb1 – c3

White defends his e-pawn and develops his knight at the same time. In his third move White could play e4–e5 or Nb1–d2, instead. Playing 3. e4 × d5 wouldn't exactly be a mistake, but it is not very ambitious. Black's reply, 3. . . . e6 × d5, would free her queen's bishop to

range the c8–h3 diagonal.

3. . . .   Ng8 – f6

Black adds to the pressure on the white e-pawn.

4. Bc1 – g5

White responds by **pinning** the black knight on f6 against the queen on d8, thereby reducing the strength of Black's attack on the white pawn.

4. . . .   Bf8 – e7

Black unpins her knight — her king is now protected both by her bishop on e7 and by her queen on d8, so she is free to move her knight.

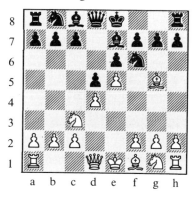

The board above shows the position after White's fifth move.

5. e4 – e5

White attacks the black knight on f6. He has no good way of keeping the pawn on e4 — if he doesn't move it, it will be captured. Now White's d- and e-pawns are fixed — their advance is blocked by the black pawns — and they will come under fire. But in compensation, White has created greater space for his other pieces to **develop**.

5.   ...   Nf6 – d7

The black knight retreats to a square from which it can support . . . c7–c5 while attacking the white e-pawn.

6.   Bg5 × e7   Qd8 × e7

White **exchanges** or trades his own **bad bishop** for Black's **good bishop**.

7.   f2 – f4

With this move White adds to his control of the e5 square. The correct placing of pawns and pieces is very important in this type of **closed position**.

The fight now shifts from the central **pawn chain** to the c- and f-files. Both players will try to undermine each other's position. Black will aim to play . . . c7–c5, hoping that White will respond with d4 × c5, thereby breaking his pawn chain. This blow will be most effective when White has a knight on c3, as now, and is unable to support his pawn chain in the center by advancing his c-pawn to c3.

The French defense has been used often by such great **masters** as Capablanca and Botvinnik.

Caro-Kann Defense — Classical System

The Caro-Kann is named after two famous 19th-century players, H. Caro and M. Kann. Its revival in popularity in this century dates from its adoption by the Soviet world champion Mikhail Botvinnik during the 1950s.

The strategic ideas behind the Caro-Kann are similar to those of the French defense. In both openings White establishes pawns on d4 and e4, which Black attempts to counteract by placing her d-pawn on d5.

As you read, play through the following sequence of moves on your own chessboard.

1. e2 – e4   c7 – c6
2. d2 – d4   d7 – d5
3. Nb1 – c3

White **develops** his queen's knight and protects the e-pawn.

3. . . .   d5 × e4

This is Black's best move. The alternative move, 3. . . . Ng8 –f6, is met by White with 4. e4–e5. This would drive the black knight to a less active square to avoid capture.

4. Nc3 × e4   Bc8 – f5

Black attacks the white knight on e4 with a developing move.

5. Ne4 – g3

White's best move in this position. Now the black bishop on f5

is under attack and must move to avoid capture.

5. . . .   Bf5 – g6

Retreating the bishop to e6 would block Black's e-pawn, making it difficult for Black to develop her king's bishop. Placing the retreating bishop on d7, on the other hand, would restrict the queen's knight, while the bishop itself would be shut in when Black plays . . . e7–e6.

The board below shows the position after Black's fifth move.

White sets a trap for the black g6 bishop in his next move, h2

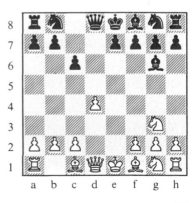

◀ ▶ **The position of the pieces** after Black's fifth move in the Caro-Kann defense. Black has been forced to retreat her bishop to g6 to escape from White's attacking knight on g3.

−h4, preparing for h4–h5. Because he is planning to **castle** queen's side, the king's-side move h2–h4 does not create a weakness near his king.

6.   h2 – h4   h7 – h6

Black creates a safe retreat for her bishop (. . . Bg6–h7) in case it comes under attack from White's h-pawn.

7.   Ng1 – f3   Nb8 – d7
8.   h4 – h5

White pursues the black bishop

positioned on the g6 square.

8.   . . .   Bg6 – h7
9.   Bf1 – d3

White hopes to trade bishops along the b1–h7 diagonal, since the black bishop is restricting White's knight on g3. Once the bishops have been removed, both sides will try to castle queen's side and to develop their remaining pieces. Black has a rather passive position and must exploit any mistakes made by White in order to win.

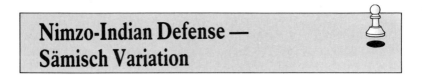

Nimzo-Indian Defense — Sämisch Variation

This opening was invented by the Latvian **grandmaster** Aron Nimzowitsch, who was one of the most original chess players of this century. He was active during the 1920s and 1930s and narrowly failed in his ambition to become world champion.

In playing style, Nimzowitsch belonged to the hypermodern school. This school held that control of the center need not be achieved only by occupying it with pawns, but that an acceptable alternative lay in allowing one's opponent to build a strong **pawn center** and then playing to undermine it.

In the Nimzo-Indian defense, White attempts to form a powerful pawn center and places his pieces behind it for the attack. Eventually, White hopes to play e2–e4. Black therefore aims her pieces toward the e4 square.

1.   d2 – d4   Ng8 – f6

Instead of using her pawns,

Black attacks the e4 square through piece **development**.

2.   c2 – c4   e7 – e6
3.   Nb1 – c3   Bf8 – b4
3.   a2 – a3

White attacks the black bishop on b4 and forces Black to **exchange**, or trade, bishop for knight. Black would waste valuable time retreating this bishop to safety on either d6 or e7.

| 4. | ... | Bb4 × c3+ |
| 5. | b2 × c3 | |

White now has **doubled pawns** on the c-file. Doubled pawns (two pawns of the same color, one in front of the other) can often be a disability. But, in this case, White hopes that the pawns will reinforce his center.

| 5. | ... | 0–0 |

Black rushes her king to safety before attacking the doubled pawns. This is a sensible plan, since White can surge forward with his central pawns and Black's king should not be left in the firing line.

| 6. | e2 – e3 | c7 – c5 |

White wants to build a pawn wall stretching from c4 to f4. Black responds by blockading the white pawn on c4 in order to prepare for her own attack.

| 7. | Bf1 – d3 | |

The board below shows the position after White's seventh move. It would be most unwise for White to take the black pawn with 7. d4×c5, instead. The gain of the black pawn is an illusion, as Black's seventh and eighth moves, . . . Nb8–a6 and Qd8–a5, would lead quickly to the capture of the white pawn on c5 by the black queen (protected by the knight on a6).

| 7. | ... | Nb8 – c6 |
| 8. | Ng1 – e2 | |

This is a better move for White than positioning his king's knight on f3, where it would block the path of his own f-pawn.

| 8. | ... | b7 – b6 |

Black opens the way for her

▶ **The position after** White's seventh move in the Sämisch variation of the Nimzo-Indian defense.

queen's bishop and prepares to play . . . Bc8–a6.

9. e3 – e4

White threatens to play Bc1–g5, **pinning** the black knight on f6 against the queen on d8. White would follow with e4–e5, attacking the black knight and possibly winning it, since the knight wouldn't be able to move without allowing the white bishop on g5 to take the black queen.

9. . . . Nf6 – e8!

Black reacts quickly and moves her knight out of danger.

10. 0–0

Both White and Black have scored brilliant wins in master games from this position. White's pieces have good scope for movement and he hopes to forge ahead with his central pawns. In turn, Black wants to blockade the position to cut down the white bishops' freedom of movement and to halt the white pawns.

In order to achieve this, Black will play . . . f7–f5, obstructing White's f-pawn and blockading the action of White's e-pawn. The black pawn on f5 will be supported by . . . g7–g6 and . . . Ne8–g7.

Black's plan is to take advantage of White's weak forward doubled pawn on c4. This wound in White's position cannot be defended by another pawn and is a target for operations such as . . . Bc8–a6 and . . . Nc6–a5.

▼ **A game of chess in a 19th-**century — a caricature by the artist George Cruikshank.

King's Indian Defense — Sämisch Variation

This opening allows White to build up a **pawn center** unchallenged. Black then unleashes a counterattack, attempting to undermine White's position with the c- and e-pawn thrusts . . . c7–c5 and . . . e7–e6 or . . . e7–e5.

▶ **The position after** White's seventh move in the Sämisch variation of the King's Indian defense.

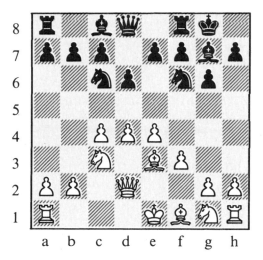

Play through the moves on your chessboard as you read.

1. d2 – d4   Ng8 – f6
2. c2 – c4   g7 – g6
3. Nb1 – c3   Bf8 – g7

Black **fianchettoes** her king's bishop, ready to apply pressure along the h8–a1 diagonal.

4. e2 – e4   d7 – d6
5. f2 – f3

This is the key move of the Sämisch variation and was developed in the 1920s by the famous German **grandmaster** Fritz Sämisch. The move reinforces White's central pawns. White intends to castle queen's side and then to storm Black's king with his king's-side pawns.

5. . . .   0–0
6. Bc1 – e3   Nb8 – c6
7. Qd1 – d2

The board above shows the position after White's seventh move.

The White maneuver Bc1–e3 and Qd1–d2 is a standard way of opposing a fianchetto formation. White's plan is to play Be3

–h6, in order to **exchange**, or trade, the fianchettoed bishop on g7: if Black responds with . . . Bg7×h6, White can recapture the piece with Qd2×h6, reestablishing the balance in **material** and positioning his queen on an aggressive square near the black king. If Black does not trade bishops on h6, White will do so on g7.

All this is part of an attacking plan that will also involve the advance of the white king's-side pawns: g2–g4, h2–h4, h4–h5, and h5×g6. Then White hopes to use his rook to continue his attack along the h-file.

Black's last move (6. . . . Nb8–c6) blocks the c-file, which is normally a disadvantage in queen's-side openings. But she will now pursue activity in the center to counter White's king's-side attack. Black will aim to play . . . e7–e5.

▼ **A game of chess between** three sisters — an engraving of a mid-16th-century painting.

Queen's Gambit Accepted

Until the latter quarter of the 19th century, it was standard practice for White to play 1. e2–e4 in international tournaments. Then 1. d2–d4 also became popular. The reply 1. . . . d7–d5 is the most natural for Black, because it prevents White from playing 2. e2–e4 to build a strong **pawn center**. Instead White plays c2–c4 in his second move and offers the c-pawn as a **gambit**, or temporary sacrifice.

If Black accepts the gambit and takes the c-pawn, she allows White to assume control of the center. But Black hopes her opponent will lose time trying to regain the pawn.

Set up your chessboard in the starting position and play through the moves as you read.

1. d2 – d4   d7 – d5
2. c2 – c4   d5 × c4

In principle, White can easily regain his lost pawn by attacking Black's pawn on c4 with his own king's bishop, after a move such as e2–e3 or e2–e4.

3. Ng1 – f3

But first White **develops** a piece. This is the most popular move with **grandmasters**, at this stage of this game.

3. . . .   Ng8 – f6

Black must develop her pieces as well. This move also prevents White from playing e2–e4 in his fourth move, as the white e-pawn would then be threatened by Black's knight on f6.

4. e2 – e3

White prepares to regain his lost pawn by using his king's bishop to play the move Bf1 × c4.

4. . . .   e7 – e6

Black wants to play . . . c7–c5 to attack White's d-pawn. Her king's bishop now defends the c5 square.

Note that it would be very dangerous for Black to try to keep her extra pawn. For example, the game could continue in this way: 4. . . . b7–b5; 5. a2–a4 c7–c6; 6. a4 × b5 c6 × b5; 7. b2–b3. If Black then takes the pawn on b3, White will continue with Bf1 × b5+ and then Qd1 × b3. This will give White a big lead in piece development, in addition to regaining his sacrificed pawn.

5. Bf1 × c4   c7 – c5
6. 0–0

The board on the next page shows the position after White's sixth move.

If White plays 6. d4 × c5 instead, this will allow the **exchange** of queens and break up

81

White's central pawns. This alternative move is often played when White wants to settle for a draw.

6.   ...   a7 – a6

Black is now threatening to play the moves . . . b7–b5 and then . . . Bc8–b7, developing her queen's bishop on the long a8–h1 diagonal. White prevents this with his seventh move.

7.   a2 – a4!   Nb8 – c6
8.   Qd1 – e2   c5 × d4
9.   Rf1 – d1

White develops his pieces in preparation for the attack. He will easily regain his pawn and will then have the more active position in addition to better control of the center.

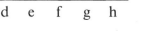

◀ **The position after** White's sixth move in the Queen's Gambit Accepted.

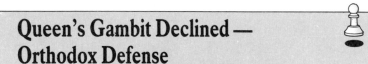

Queen's Gambit Declined — Orthodox Defense

Of course, Black doesn't have to accept White's c-pawn as a **gambit**. Instead, Black can concentrate on building up her own **pawn center** and **developing** her pieces.

Set up your chessboard and pieces in the starting position again, and play through the moves of this opening variation as you read.

1.   d2 – d4   d7 – d5
2.   c2 – c4   e7 – e6

Black defends her d-pawn. This is the most popular way for

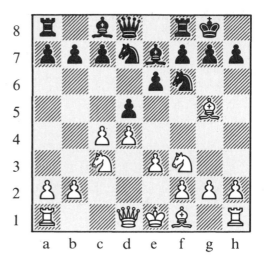

► **The position after** Black's sixth move in the Orthodox defense of the Queen's Gambit Declined.

Black to decline the gambit, although 2. ... c7–c6 is a reasonable alternative.

The move 2. ... Ng8–f6 would be a mistake, since it allows White to develop a powerful center. The game would continue with 3. c4 × d5 Nf6 × d5 and 4. e2–e4, and the black knight on d5 would have to retreat to avoid capture (e4 × Nd5).

3. Nb1 – c3   Ng8 – f6
4. Bc1 – g5

White develops his attack on the d5 square, by **pinning** the black f6 knight against the queen. The black knight cannot now move to protect the d-pawn.

4. ...   Bf8 – e7

Black advances her king's bishop to protect her queen, releasing the pin. The f6 knight is now free to move without open-

ing the black queen to capture by White's bishop on g5.

5. Ng1 – f3   0–0

Both sides make developing moves, with Black **castling** king's side.

6. e2 – e3

White's king's bishop is best placed on d3 in this position.

6. ...   Nb8 – d7

Black supports the knight on f6. It would be a mistake to play 6. ... Nb8–c6, since it blocks the black c-pawn. (The board above shows the current position.)

7. Ra1 – c1

White can open the c-file later by playing c4 × d5, setting his rook free to range along the file.

7. ...   c7 – c6

Black gives her d-pawn extra

protection. Black is preparing to free her position by **exchanging** pieces.

8. Bf1 – d3   d5 × c4!
9. Bd3 × c4   Nf6 – d5!

White's g5 bishop now has no retreat available to it — it is vulnerable to capture whichever way it moves. The bishops are therefore exchanged (Bg5 × e7 and . . . Qd8 × e7), and Black then exchanges knights by playing . . . Nd5 × c3, with White responding with either b2 × c3 or Rc1 × c3.

King's Gambit Accepted

During the 19th century the King's Gambit was one of the most popular openings. White offers to sacrifice his f-pawn on his second move, with the aim of opening up assault lines against the black king. As opening theory developed, however, players discovered that Black can usually neutralize White's attack by following a sensible plan of **development**.

At **master** level it is now rare to see players choose to employ this opening, but at club level it is still popular with those players who opt for dynamic tactical positions.

Play through the following moves as you read.

1. e2 – e4   e7 – e5
2. f2 – f4

White offers his f-pawn as a **gambit**. White intends to open the f-file for an assault on the weak f7 square (see page 68).

2. . . .   e5 × f4
3. Ng1 – f3

This is White's best move, stopping Black from giving **check** with . . . Qd8–h4+. It also furthers White's strategy of developing his king's-side pieces.

3. . . .   g7 – g5

Black supports her pawn on f4.

White develops his king's-side pieces further in his next move and points his bishop at the key f7 square, using the a2–g8 diagonal.

4. Bf1 – c4   d7 – d6

Black opens the c8–h3 diagonal for her queen's bishop and stops the white king's knight from advancing to e5, where it would add to the pressure on f7.

5. 0–0

The white rook goes to f1 where it adds to the pressure on f7. White is now three **tempi**, or moves, ahead of Black in development, since he has already developed his knight from g1 and his bishop from f1, in addition to **castling**.

5. . . .   h7 – h6

Black supports her pawn on g5 and prevents White from using his knight to launch a dangerous attack on the king's side.

6. d2 – d4   Bf8 – g7

White has completed a powerful **pawn center**, as the board below shows. Now he can unleash the attack against the black king.

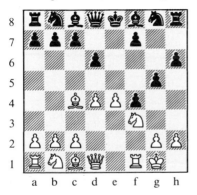

Black's sixth move, . . . Bf8 –g7, is better than placing her bishop on e7. White may try to open up the position by playing e4–e5, and now the black bishop covers that square along the a1–h8 diagonal.

7. c2 – c3

White supports his d-pawn and prepares for the move Qd1–b3, which will intensify the attack on f7 along the a2–g8 diagonal.

7. . . .   Nb8 – c6
8. g2 – g3!

White is ready to attack. He will bring his queen's knight over to the attack by developing it to d2. He will then smash through Black's king's-side defenses by opening the f-file, if necessary by sacrificing a knight.

Black needs to play very carefully in order to repulse the onslaught. If she does, her extra **material** will tell in her favor.

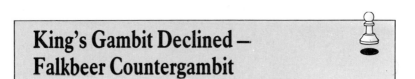

King's Gambit Declined – Falkbeer Countergambit

This opening variation is just one of the ways Black can decline White's **gambit** of his f-pawn.

1. e2 – e4   e7 – e5
2. f2 – f4   d7 – d5

Black ignores White's gambit and offers her own d-pawn as a

temporary sacrifice. She has freed both of her bishops for action and will have no problems in **developing** her own pieces.

3. e4 × d5

White accepts the gambit. Why doesn't he play f4 × e5 instead?

Because Black's reply, . . . Qd8 −h4+, would open an unstoppable assault on his king. For example, the game could continue with 4. g2−g3 Qh4×e4+, followed by 5. . . . Qe4×h1, winning a rook (a **major piece**). An alternative sequence of moves would be 4. Ke1−e2 Qh4 −e4+ and 5. Ke2−f2 Bf8−c5+, hounding White's king out into the open. Black would win the game soon after this sequence.

3.   . . .   e5 – e4

This move cramps White's position by preventing him from developing his king's knight to the f3 square.

4.   d2 – d3

White attacks Black's e-pawn.

4.   . . .   Ng8 – f6

For Black to try to win back the pawn with the alternative move,

4.   . . . Qd8×d5, would lead to a complicated variation of this opening, which would not benefit her in the long run.

5.   d3 × e4   Nf6 × e4

The board below shows the position after Black's fifth move. Black now threatens a strong attack, with 6. . . . Qd8 −h4+ followed by 7. g2−g3 Ne4×g3.

6.   Ng1 – f3   Bf8 – c5

Black directs her king's bishop against White's weak spot on f2 (see page 68).

7.   Qd1 – e2

White puts pressure on the e-file — Black's knight on e4 is now **pinned** against her king. White will continue to develop his pieces, putting his queen's knight on c3 and his queen's bishop on e3.

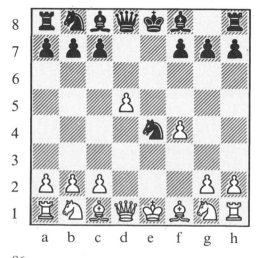

◀ **The position after** Black's fifth move in the Falkbeer Countergambit, a variation of the King's Gambit Declined.

86

English Opening

This is one of the most successful of the opening systems developed by the hypermodern school of the 1920s. It is a favorite of Gary Kasparov. White plays 1. c2–c4, striking from the **flank** at d5. Later, White hopes to dominate this square with his pieces.

Black can choose to respond by imitating White's moves, as in the variation given here, in which case the two armies do not engage until the opening phase is well under way.

1. c2 – c4   c7 – c5
2. Nb1 – c3

White doubles his attack on the d5 square.

2. . . .   Nb8 – c6

Black retaliates by putting pressure on the d4 square.

3. g2 – g3

White prepares to **fianchetto** his king's bishop to g2. From g2, this bishop will be pointing at d5 along the long diagonal.

3. . . .   g7 – g6
4. Bf1 – g2   Bf8 – g7

Both players fianchetto their king's bishop.

5. Ng1 – f3   Ng8 – f6

The knights are **developed**. The board below shows the position after Black's fifth move.

Both sides will continue by **castling** king's side, and then White will play d2–d4, freeing his queen's bishop. He will then be able to complete his piece development.

▶ **The position after** Black's fifth move in the English Opening.

Réti Opening

This is another **flank** opening and it was made popular by the Hungarian grandmaster Richard Réti, one of the leading exponents of the hypermodern school.

The Réti opening is a valuable weapon for cautious players, who want to keep a tight rein on their pieces.

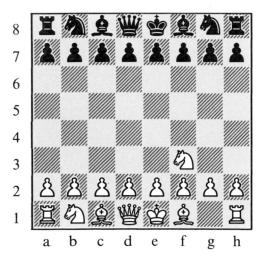

◄ **The position after** White's first move in the Réti opening. The move Ng1–f3 is a popular and safe opening play.

The board above shows the position of the pieces after White's first move.

1.   Ng1 – f3

This is a popular and safe opening. It is particularly apt against beginners, who sometimes blunder a pawn immediately with the response 1. . . . e7–e5?, allowing 2. Nf3×e5. The following move is more rational.

1.   . . .   d7 – d5
2.   c2 – c4   d5 × c4
3.   Nb1 – a3

White can now regain the pawn

with 4. Na3×c4. An alternative would be to play 3. Qd1–a4 +, followed by Qa4×c4.

Another variation of the Réti opening is:

1.   Ng1 – f3   Ng8 – f6
2.   g2 – g3   c7 – c5
3.   Bf1 – g2   e7 – e6
4.   0–0   d7 – d5
5.   d2 – d3   Nb8 – c6
6.   Nb1 – d2

The board opposite shows the position at this stage.

White follows up with expansion into the center, based on the move e2–e4.

► **The position after** White's sixth move in the Réti opening. White is ready to push into the center, beginning with e2–e4.

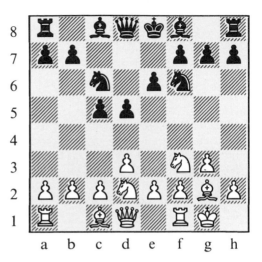

▼ **Many towns and** cities throughout the world have giant open-air chessboards and pieces. This game is being played in Baden-Baden, in West Germany.

5: The Middle Game

When most of the chess pieces have been **developed** the game enters its second phase, the middle game. This is the least charted area of chess and it is uniquely difficult to play.

The various opening strategies have been extensively analyzed and there are thousands of books that will tell you how to play the first few moves of a game. Some books on chess openings will even take you as far as move 25, or further.

Many of the endgames have also been studied thoroughly. Certain endings are known to be won or drawn by following a set series of moves or ideas, and strategy in the endgame is often devoted to

achieving a known position, from which a standard technique will guarantee success.

In the middle game, however, there are few recurring sequences of winning moves. The pieces are actively deployed on the board by this stage, and the relationship between them is very much more complex than during other phases of the game. There are so many possibilities in the middle game that no number of books can contain everything you need to know to be a strong player — you are largely on your own.

You can improve the technique of your middle game by studying the games of the great players and by playing as many games as you can. There are also some valuable strategic guidelines that will help you to avoid potential weaknesses in your position and to build up advantages. These are discussed in the remainder of this chapter.

Mobility

The word "mobility" is used in chess to mean the freedom of action of the chess pieces. Your mobility can be measured by the number of squares that your pieces are attacking, including those occupied by your opponent. Adding up the number of squares your pieces are attacking will tell you how much mobility you have.

In general, the player with a big advantage in piece mobility has the better position, since the pieces are more flexible and can move around the board more freely. Bear in mind that pieces placed on or near the center of the board usually have greater mobility than those tucked away on the edges.

King Safety

In the opening and the middle game, the king should be carefully guarded. Normally, this means moving it away from the central files, where it can be easily attacked by the enemy queen and rooks.

The best way of securing the king's safety is to **castle** queen's side or king's side. The pawns in front of the castled king should be kept in a fairly tight formation on their 2nd or 3rd ranks. Overextending the pawns to their 4th rank or beyond will make them vulnerable to attack in the middle game.

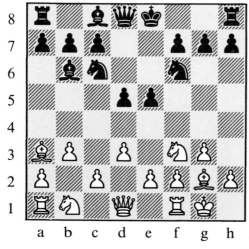

◀ **Castling is the best** way of securing the king's safety. Here, the white king has castled and is well protected by pawns, as well as by a knight and a bishop.

On the board at the bottom of the preceding page, the white king is safely castled, with a solid phalanx of pawns in front of it and protection from both the g2 bishop and the f3 knight.

Black's king, on the other hand, hasn't yet castled and is looking rather exposed on the central file. Furthermore, the white bishop on a3 is attacking the f8 square, which is preventing Black from castling king's side. (Black has already moved her queen's rook from a8 and back again, and so she cannot castle queen's side.)

Unless Black castles quickly, her king will come under fierce attack. Black's best move is . . . Nc6–e7, which will block the line of attack of the white bishop on a3 and allow Black to castle on her next move.

In the game shown on the board below, both players have castled king's side. Since castling, White has moved his king g1–h1 and launched an attack against Black's king. Part of White's attack was to rush up the board using his king's-side pawns. This can be a double-edged strategy, and here it has left White's king very exposed. If the attack doesn't work quickly, Black will be able to move her queen and some of her other pieces right into the camp of White's king, with devastating effect.

White's attack hasn't yet achieved its aim of disrupting the black king's position, so Black has time to counterattack. She now decides to take a loss in **material** in the hope of future gains, sacrificing a **major piece** for a **minor piece** — a rook for a knight. This is even stronger than taking the white e-pawn, a possible alternative.

▶ **Although White has** castled his king here, the pawn attack he has since launched on the black king has left his own king looking rather exposed. (This position is also illustrated in the photograph on pages 90–91.)

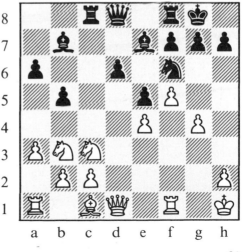

Set your chess pieces up in the position illustrated on the board on page 93, and play through the following sequence of moves as you read.

1.   . . .   Rc8 × c3!
2.   b2 × c3   Nf6 × e4

Black gives up a rook but in return gains a knight and a pawn. This is a sacrifice in material roughly equal in value to one pawn (see "Values of the Pieces," page 45). But Black has already achieved something in return for her loss.

Before Black made these moves, the white king was protected from the black bishop on b7 by the white pawn on e4, backed by the knight on c3. Black has removed both these white pieces and the white king has come under fire because it doesn't have a safe shield of pawns to hide behind. .

Now Black is threatening to play . . . Ne4–f2+, and this **discovered check** (White's king will be in check from Black's bishop on b7) will win the game. This is because the black knight will be attacking the white queen and when White moves his king out of check his queen will be captured.

White decides to move his king first.

3.   Kh1 – g1   Qd8 – b6+!

Black seals White's fate. White cannot safely escape from the check by putting his knight or queen on d4, because Black is already attacking the d4 square with her e-pawn.

If, on the other hand, White blocks the check by moving his queen's bishop to e3, the black queen will capture it and the white king will still be in check. And if White moves his king back to h1 again, then . . . Ne4–g3 would be **checkmate**.

White now moves his rook in a vain attempt to stop the attack.

4.   Rf1 – f2   Qb6 × f2+
5.   Kg1 – h1   Ne4 – g3
                          checkmate

A pretty **double check** — the white king is in check both to the black knight on g3 and to the bishop on b7. The game is over and Black has won.

Pawn Structure

Some pawn structures are weak and some are strong, and careful positioning and handling of the pawns is vital in the middle game. You will discover that a sound pawn formation can mean the difference between winning and losing a game. Some examples of the various pawn structures follow on the next few pages.

Doubled pawns

This is when two pawns of the same color are positioned one in front of the other on the same file. On the board below, the white pawns on the c-file are doubled.

Doubled pawns are generally regarded as a weakness, since they are much more difficult to defend than pawns on adjacent files. When pawns are one in front of the other on adjacent files — say, on squares c3 and d4 — the one behind can defend the one in front. Because pawns capture by moving diagonally, this is impossible when pawns are doubled.

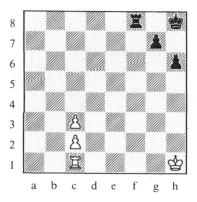

On the board above, for example, it is Black's turn to move, and she can win the forward c-pawn simply by attacking it with the rook move . . . Rf8–c8. White is powerless to save his pawn on c3, since the pawn on c2 cannot defend it, and Black will take it even if it advances to c4.

In some cases doubled pawns have advantages, because they can provide extra cover for important central squares. On the board illustrated below, Black's doubled pawns on c7 and c6 are not a significant weakness because they are helping to control the important d6 and d5 squares.

▶ **Although usually a weakness**, in some cases doubled pawns have their advantages. Here, Black's doubled pawns on c7 and c6 are covering the important central squares, d6 and d5.

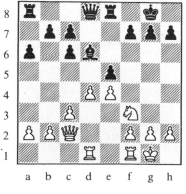

Isolated pawns

A pawn is isolated when it isn't supported by pawns on the files adjacent to it. On the board below, the white d-pawn is isolated and has no support from pawns in the c- and e-files.

An isolated pawn is also weak because it makes it difficult to attack the square in front of it. An enemy piece placed on the square in front of it cannot be driven away by advancing a neighboring pawn to threaten it.

If it were White's turn to move on the board below, he would probably advance his isolated pawn from d4 to d5, attacking Black's knight on c6 and seizing the initiative. But it is Black's move here, and she starts to lay siege to the isolated pawn.

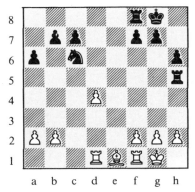

Set your pieces up in the position shown on the board above and follow the moves as you read.

The first stage of Black's siege is to block the isolated white pawn.

1. . . .   Rh5 – d5

Now the white d-pawn cannot advance. The pawn is being attacked by two of Black's pieces (it is already threatened by the black knight on c6) and is defended only once (by the rook

on d1). White must bring up reinforcements.

2. Be1 – c3   Rf8 – d8

Again Black has more pieces attacking the isolated pawn on d4 than White has defending it. It looks as though there isn't any way of saving the pawn — or is there?

3. Rd1 – d3

This move doesn't add to the defense of d4, but it now appears as though White is setting a trap. Can Black safely capture the pawn on d4?

3. . . .   Nc6 × d4
4. Rf1 – d1

Has White saved the day by doubling the attack on the black knight? After all, if the knight retreats — to c6, e6 or f5, for example — White will simply capture the black rook on d5. Both of the white rooks are attacking d5, whereas only one black rook is defending it.

Black's fourth move is the key to her strategy in capturing the isolated d-pawn.

4.   . . .   Nd4 – e2 + !

Black moves her knight to safety and at the same time gives **check**. Because White .must move to escape the check, he doesn't have enough time to win the black rook on d5. Indeed, the move results in Black winning even more **material**.

5.   Kg1 – f1   Ne2 × c3

If White now moves to recapture the knight, Black will capture on d3 and win a **major piece**, the rook.

6.   Rd3 × d5   Rd8 × d5
7.   Rd1 × d5   Nc3 × d5

Black is a knight and a pawn ahead of White in material.

Pawns that are both doubled *and* isolated are an even greater weakness than pawns that are either isolated or doubled. This is evident in the variation on page 77, where Black quickly wins the pawn on c3. Triple isolated pawns are even more fatal to their owner, as the game that follows shows.

Set up your chess pieces in the position illustrated on the board above right and follow the moves as you read. You'll discover that the triple isolated black pawns on c5, c6, and c7 are really no better than one pawn, as White quickly mops up

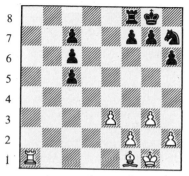

two of them with his rook and bishop.

1.   Ra1 – c1

There goes the first pawn. Black has no way whatsoever of defending the pawn on c5.

1.   . . .   Rf8 – e8
2.   Rc1 × c5

White is now attacking the c6 pawn.

2.   . . .   Re8 – e6

Black defends the pawn on c6.

3.   Bf1 – g2

White doubles the attack on the c6 pawn. Black now has no way to save this pawn.

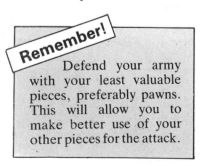

Remember!

Defend your army with your least valuable pieces, preferably pawns. This will allow you to make better use of your other pieces for the attack.

Passed pawns

A passed pawn is one whose forward march cannot be stopped by an enemy pawn, either on the same file or on an adjacent file. On the board below, the white e-pawn is a passed pawn. There is no black pawn on the e-file to block its path, nor are there black pawns at d7 or f7 to prevent its advance from e5 to e6.

It is much easier to promote a passed pawn than an ordinary pawn, and you will learn how to do this in the next chapter, "The Endgame" (see pages 118–19). Often, therefore, a passed pawn is a very valuable asset.

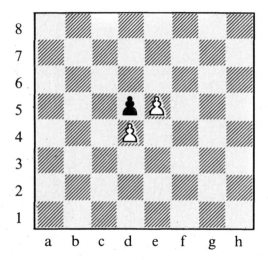

◄ **The white e-pawn** is a passed pawn here, because there are no black pawns on the same or adjacent files to block its forward march.

Hanging pawns

The term "hanging pawns" was coined by Wilhelm Steinitz, who was world champion from 1886 to 1894. It refers to two pawns in neighboring files, which are neither **passed** nor opposed by an enemy pawn on the same file.

The white d- and e-pawns on the board opposite are hanging pawns. Neither of them is a passed pawn — the black pawns on c7 and f7 protect the d- and e-files, preventing the white pawns' advance — nor are they opposed by enemy pawns on the same file.

Hanging pawns are a notorious double-edged weapon. They are

pronc to attack, because although they each have a pawn on an adjacent file, they cannot support each other at the same time. If one pawn advances, the pawn that is left behind has no support. On the other hand, hanging pawns do have some advantages in terms of control of space and flexibility in the way they advance.

▶ **Here, the white** d- and e-pawns are hanging pawns. They are not passed pawns, as Black has pawns on the adjacent c- and f-files, nor are they opposed by enemy pawns on their files.

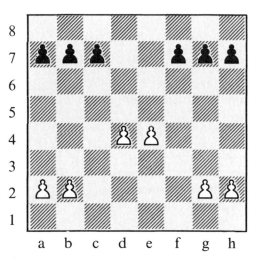

▼ **World Champion** from 1886 to 1894, and the person who coined the term "hanging pawns," Wilhelm Steinitz is sitting to the left of the chessboard in this 19th-century engraving.

Backward pawns

A backward pawn is one that has been left behind by its neighbors and can no longer rely on their support against attack by an enemy piece. The white c-pawn is backward on the board below, for example.

There are few advantages to having a backward pawn — indeed, it is the worst thing that can happen to a pawn. If the black pawns weren't on b4 and d4 on the board below, White would be able to iron out his pawn structure by advancing his backward pawn to c3. But White cannot afford to play c2–c3, as his pawn could then be taken by either of the black pawns on the adjacent files. And if White advances his pawn to c4 it will also be taken — **en passant**, again by either of the black pawns. (Remember that if a pawn moves from its 2nd to its 4th rank in one turn, it can be captured by an enemy pawn positioned on an adjacent file just as if it had advanced only to its 3rd rank.) White's backward pawn is therefore fixed, as a permanent weakness.

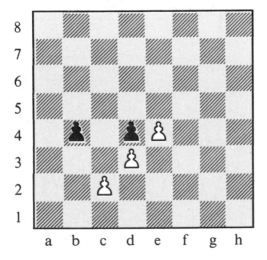

◀ **The white c-pawn** on this board is a backward pawn — it has been left behind by its neighbors and can no longer rely on their protection.

Another disadvantage of having a backward pawn is that the square immediately in front of it can often be safely occupied by an enemy piece, as there are no pawns to defend the square. On the board above, Black could usefully post a knight or some other piece on c3, knowing that White has no pawns on b2 or d2 to threaten the c3 square.

Closed and Open Files

A file is closed when a white and a black pawn are stationed on it. An open file has no pawns on it.

An open file can be used to advantage, because a rook can operate along it without the pawns getting in the way. Try to place your rooks on open files, and if there is only one file open, think about lining up both rooks on it, one in front of the other. These rooks will then be ready to penetrate the heart of the enemy camp at an appropriate moment.

A semi-open file is one that is occupied by only one pawn. This type of file is often an advantage to the player who doesn't have a pawn on it, because that player's own rooks and queen can roam the file without fear of opposition from enemy rooks. It is particularly useful to have your rook or queen on a semi-open file if there is an enemy **backward** or **isolated pawn** on it, since you will find that it is usually easier for you to attack the pawn than it is for your opponent to defend it.

▶ **On this board, the** files a, b, e, f, and g are closed. The h-file is open, while the c-file and the d-file are semi-open.

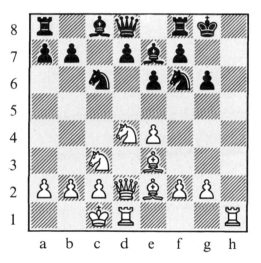

With the pieces in the position illustrated on the board above, the h-file is open — there aren't any pawns along the file — and White would win with an attack down this file. The c-file is semi-open, since only White retains a c-pawn. The d-file is also semi-open — Black has a d-pawn while White's has been captured. The other five files are all closed at this stage of the game.

Bad and Good Bishops

At the beginning of a game each player has two bishops: one on a light-colored square and one on a dark-colored square. A bad bishop is one that is hemmed in by its own pawns, positioned on the same color square as itself. A good bishop is one that isn't. In the middle game a bad bishop can sometimes be used defensively, but in the endgame it will often watch helplessly as an enemy knight or a good bishop roams the board wreaking havoc.

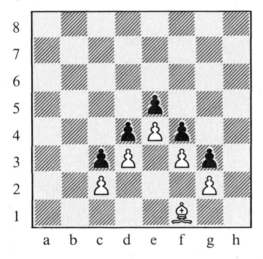

◄ ▼ **Here, the white** bishop on f1 is a bad bishop. It has absolutely no future, as the diagonals f1–a6 and f1–h3 are blocked by its own pawns which, like itself, are on light-colored squares.

Winning Tactics

There are various tricks of the chess trade that can often be employed during the middle game with decisive effect. The three most important are the fork, the skewer, and the pin.

The fork

On the chessboard, a fork is a move that attacks more than one enemy piece. The most common fork is that made by the knight. This piece can attack the king and the queen at the same time without coming under attack itself, as the board below shows. Here, the white king is in check and must move away from f1. The black knight on e3 will then take the queen on d1.

▶ **The most common** fork is that made by the knight, which can attack the king and the queen at the same time without coming under fire itself.

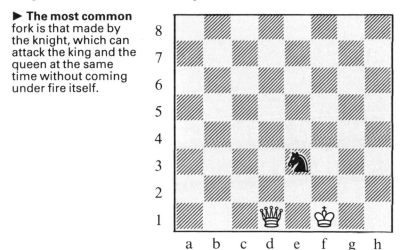

Another type of fork is commonly seen in the opening when beginners, in particular, can fall prey to a pawn maneuver that forks both a knight and a bishop. The example at the top of the next page, from the popular Ruy Lopez opening (see also pages 69–71), is typical. Inexperienced players conscientiously develop their bishops and knights during the opening, according to well-established advice, but are then hit by a sudden advance of enemy pawns that ends in a fork of two pieces.

Set up your chessboard and pieces in the starting position and play through the following opening sequence.

1.	e2 – e4	e7 – e5
2.	Ng1 – f3	Nb8 – c6
3.	Bf1 – b5	Bf8 – c5

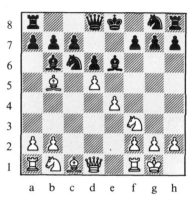

Both Black and White have now developed a knight and a bishop. White is ready to castle.

4.	0–0	d7 – d6
5.	c2 – c3	Bc8 – e6
6.	d2 – d4	e5 × d4
7.	c3 × d4	Bc5 – b6
8.	d4 – d5	

White's eighth move forks the black knight on c6 and the black bishop on e6. The board above reveals the full extent of this disaster for Black.

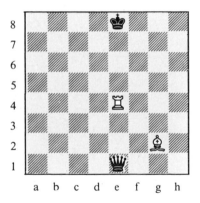

◀ **Here is another example of a** fork. In this case, it is the white rook on e4 that has the black king and queen in fork — it is attacking both pieces. If the black queen takes the rook, the white bishop on g2 will take the queen.

The skewer

This is a move that exploits the position of two enemy pieces on the same rank, file, or diagonal.

On the board at the top of the page opposite, the white bishop on a1 is attacking the black king on g7 along the long a1–h8 diagonal. Moving the black king to another square will protect it, but the white bishop will then take the queen on h8.

White's check can also be blocked by the rook move . . . f8–f6, shielding the king, but White will then take the rook on f6 with his bishop. In return, Black will take the white bishop with his king, but White will have won a **major piece** for the loss of a **minor piece**. Always watch out for skewers if your opponent's king and queen are positioned close to each other.

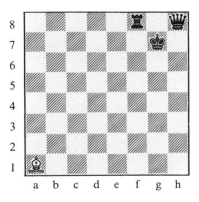

The pin

Like the skewer, the pin relies on two enemy pieces that are lined up on the same rank, file, or diagonal. In a pin, however, the attacked (or pinned) piece cannot escape, because it is shielding either the king or a much stronger piece than itself.

On the board below, the black queen is under attack from the white rook on e1. It cannot move out of the way, because the black king would then be in **check**. It could take the white rook, but White will recapture it with the d1 rook, thereby gaining an enormous advantage in **material**.

▶ **Here, the black** queen is pinned against the king. The queen cannot move out of the way, because the king would then be in check.

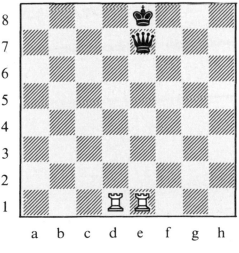

Here are some chess positions to test your awareness of forks, skewers, and pins. In each case, it is White's turn to move next. List your answers for all three boards.

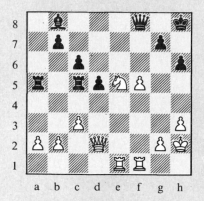

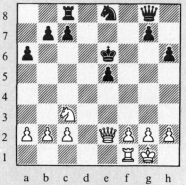

▲ **What move can White make** from this position to fork two of Black's pieces?

▲ **Two different skewers are** possible here. Can you spot them both?

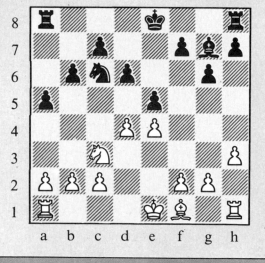

◄ **What move can** White make to set up a pin? What will happen after he has done this?

Answers on page 111

6: The Endgame

When most of the pieces have been exchanged, the final phase of the game is entered. The endgame is well documented, and certain endings are known to be wins for one side or the other. Some endings are also known to be automatic draws. Even so, play during the endgame requires great accuracy, and a single wrong move can throw away a winning position.

How to Draw

Some endings are drawn because neither side has enough **material** to win. King and knight against a king, for example, is a draw, because the extra knight is insufficient to deliver **checkmate**. Try to set up a checkmating position in which one side has a king and a knight while the other has a **lone king**. You will soon discover that checkmate is impossible. Even with a king and two knights against a lone king, you will win only if your opponent defends very badly indeed. Such a position is so difficult that your opponent with the lone king will really need to help you if you are to win with a king and two knights!

Draws can be achieved in the following ways:

- By agreement. If both players agree to a draw, the point is shared, half to each of them. (Remember that in competition chess a win counts for one point.)
- By repetition of position (including **perpetual check**). If a position is repeated three times *with the same player having the right to move*, then the game is drawn. In a serious game, the player who wishes to claim a draw in this way must do so *before* making the move that will repeat the position for the third time.
- By the 50-move rule. If both sides have played 50 successive moves without advancing a pawn or making a capture, the game is normally drawn. There are a few exceptions to this rule, but you won't need to worry about them until you are a master-strength player.
- By **stalemate** (see pages 61–63). If the player whose turn it is to move is *not* in check and has no **legal moves** available, then the player has been stalemated and the game is drawn.

Repetition of position

The most common way for a draw to occur by repetition of position is for both players to move the same pieces backward and forward, as the game that follows illustrates. With the pieces in the position shown on the board below, White is a long way behind in **material** (he is a queen and a bishop down). But it is White's turn to move and he can force a draw within a few moves.

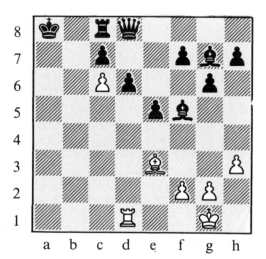

◀ ▶ **It is White's turn** to move here, and he can easily force a draw by threefold repetition of position. (The photograph opposite also illustrates this position.)

Set your board up in the position illustrated above and follow the moves as you read.

1. Rd1 – a1 +   Ka8 – b8

This is Black's only possible move, since the white pawn at c6 prevents the black king from moving to the b7 square.

2. Be3 – a7 +   Kb8 – a8
3. Ba7 – e3 +

The black king is in check to the white rook on a1 for the second time. The first time this position occurred was after White's rook

move Rd1–a1 +. It is not important that the second time the position was reached it was by a different move. It is repetition of *position* that counts.

3. . . .   Ka8 – b8
4. Be3 – a7 +   Kb8 – a8

White can now claim a draw by announcing that he intends to play Ba7–e3, and that this move will bring about a position that has occurred twice before, forcing Black to move in all three cases. The game is therefore drawn between the two players.

Perpetual check

This is a position when one of the players can give check move after move after move — thus the term "perpetual." At the same time, no matter how hard the opposing player tries to avoid the checks it is impossible to escape, as the example that follows on the next page illustrates.

With the pieces in the position shown on the board on page 110, you can see that Black has an enormous advantage in material —

she is two rooks and two bishops ahead. But Black's own king is being harassed by White's queen. Wherever the black king moves the white queen will be able to find a safe square from which to give check. Black will never be able to escape from the checks, so the game will be drawn.

Eventually, White would be able to claim a draw by claiming threefold repetition of position, but in this case it is easy to see that because the series of checks can go on forever the two players would probably agree to a draw long before White does this. Set your chess pieces up in the position illustrated on the board below and try out the moves for yourself — you will soon discover that for Black to escape from check is impossible.

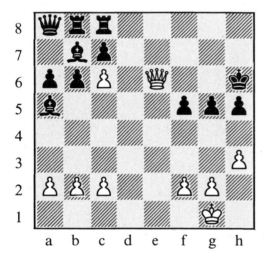

◄ **Despite Black's** advantage in material, she will draw this game by perpetual check. The black king is in a very vulnerable position and won't be able to escape the white queen's checks.

Ground rules for the endgame

- If you are a pawn ahead, exchange pieces not pawns.
- If you are a pawn down, exchange pawns not pieces.
- If you have a **passed pawn**, try to promote it. If your opponent has a passed pawn, try to block its progress.
- Don't forget to use your king. In the endgame it is a strong and active piece.

What is the winning fork?

Did you think it was Ne5–g6+, forking the black king and queen? A nice idea, but if White moves this knight he is himself in check from the black bishop on b8. Yes, the knight on e5 is **pinned** against the white king.

The correct move is b2–b4, forking both of Black's rooks. Whichever rook moves first, White can capture the other one with his pawn on b4.

Which are the skewer twins?

White's queen on e2 is the crucial attacking piece in this position. If it moves to g4 it will give check to the black king, and when the king moves out of check, the white queen can capture the black rook on c8.

Even better, however, is a different queen check, this time on the c4 square. After White plays Qe2–c4+, Black must again move her king out of check, whereupon the white queen will snatch the black queen on g8.

Where is the pin?

White can pin the black knight on c6 against the black king on e8 by moving out his bishop. After this move, Bf1–b5, the black knight on c6 is under attack and isn't yet defended. The knight cannot move, because to do so would leave the black king in check from the white bishop on b5. Black must defend the knight in the only way possible — by advancing her king to d7. Did you spot this move, . . . Ke8–d7? And if so, did you work out how White should continue? White's correct reply is now d4–d5, attacking the knight again. This time the knight cannot be defended, and because it's pinned it cannot move, so White will be able to capture it on his next turn.

The Opposition

Whenever the kings are in the position illustrated on the board below — facing each other on the same file, separated by only one square — whoever made the last move is said to have the opposition. The side with the opposition can limit the moves available to the enemy king, and in many endgames the opposition can play a decisive role.

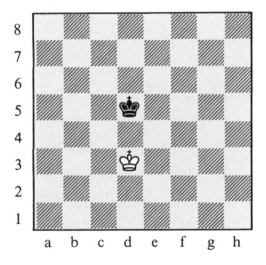

◄ **When the kings** face each other on the same file, separated by only one square as here, whoever made the last move has the opposition.

Queening a Pawn

One of the most common themes of the endgame is the attempt to **promote** a pawn. Usually, the pawn is promoted to a queen.

With the pieces in the position illustrated on the board at the top of the page opposite, White will aim to queen his pawn on the d8 square. Black will lose unless she can control the queening square at the crucial moment, thereby forcing a draw. In theory White has won, but careful play will be necessary to secure the win.

The correct technique is for White to leave his pawn where it is and to concentrate on gaining the **opposition** and using it to drive Black's king away from the vital d8 square. This must be done carefully to avoid giving Black the opposition, which would change everything and allow her to draw.

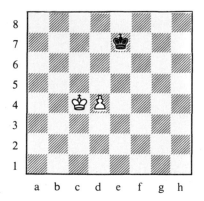

Set your pieces up in the above position and follow the moves as you read. There is only one move that will guarantee a win for White.

1. Kc4 – c5   Ke7 – d7
2. Kc5 – d5

White gains the opposition. During the next few moves you will see why the opposition is so important.

2. ...   Kd7 – e7

Alternative moves by Black illustrate the hopelessness of her position. If instead Black plays 2. . . . Kd7–c7, then White will regain the opposition with 3. Kd5–e6 Kc7–d8 and 4. Ke6–d6. Black's reply, 4. . . . Kd8–e8, would be answered by 5. Kd6–c7. Now Black cannot control the d8 square (remember that it is **illegal** to move into **check**). The white pawn can rush up the d-file to promote.

If, on the other hand, Black plays 2. . . . Kd7–d8, White can advance his king and keep the opposition. White's third move, Kd5–d6, reaches the same position as in the variation just analyzed.

But in the variation we are following, White takes his king off the d-file.

3. Kd5 – c6   Ke7 – d8
4. Kc6 – d6

White has the opposition again. Black must move to either c8 or e8, allowing White's king to reach one of the crucial squares e7 or c7.

4. ...   Kd8 – e8
5. Kd6 – c7

Black no longer controls d8 and the white pawn can advance unhindered.

5. ...   Ke8 – e7
6. d4 – d5   Ke7 – e8
7. d5 – d6   Ke8 – f7
8. d6 – d7   Kf7 – e6
9. d7 – d8 = (Q)

Black should now **resign**, since king and queen against a **lone king** (see page 123) will be an easy win for White.

Now set up your board in the above position again and follow another sequence of moves to see what would happen if White had made a mistake and played a different move instead of 1. Kc4–c5. What will happen, for instance, if White moves his king to d5?

1. Kc4 – d5??   Ke7 – d7!

Now Black has the opposition.

White moves his king again:

2. Kd5 – c5   Kd7 – c7

White cannot progress toward controlling the d8 square with his king, so his only hope is to advance the pawn.

3. d4 – d5   Kc7 – d7
4. d5 – d6   Kd7 – d8
5. Kc5 – c6   Kd8 – c8
6. d6 – d7 +   Kc8 – d8

The board right shows the position after Black's sixth move.

White must now choose between two evils. If he moves his king away from the defense of the pawn, Black will take the pawn and secure a draw. The only move that protects it is 7. Kc6–d6, which leaves Black unable to move her king without placing it in check. This is a **stalemate**, also a draw. White has thrown away half a point with one incautious move.

The diagram above also illustrates the position **zugzwang**, in which a player is at a disadvantage simply because it is his or her turn to move and for no other reason. In this game White draws only because on his seventh move he will either lose his extra pawn or give stalemate. Black would lose if it were her turn to move, but only because she must vacate the pawn promotion square, d8.

Queening a Rook's Pawn

This next example highlights the special difficulty that is posed by the rook's pawn (the a-pawn or the h-pawn). In the position shown right Black will draw even if White gains the **opposition**, as the black king cannot be forced away from the queening square, h8.

1. Kf5 – g6

White gains the opposition. As

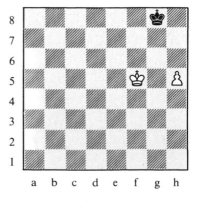

114

the following moves reveal, however, the opposition is of no help to White in this position.

1.	. . .	Kg8 – h8
2.	Kg6 – h6	Kh8 – g8
3.	Kh6 – g6	

Now you can probably understand White's difficulty. Black cannot be outflanked because White has run out of room to maneuver.

3.	. . .	Kg8 – h8
4.	h5 – h6	Kh8 – g8
5.	h6 – h7 +	Kg8 – h8
6.	Kg6 – h6 stalemate	

The game is a draw, with half a point to each player.

If White has an extra bishop in this type of ending, the outcome of the game hinges on whether the bishop is on a light square or a dark square.

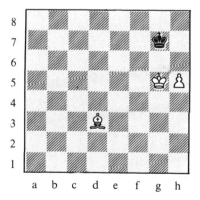

On the board above, the light-squared bishop is of no use to White, because it cannot control the vital queening square, h8. A dark-squared bishop, on the other hand, could check the black king when it reaches h8 and drive it away from the square. This tactic could be followed by the bishop giving cover to the pawn when it reaches the h8 square and queens.

The following sequence illustrates how useless the light-squared bishop would be. Set your pieces up in the position shown below left and follow the moves as you read.

1.	h5 – h6 +	Kg7 – h8
2.	Kg5 – g6	Kh8 – g8
3.	Bd3 – c4 +	Kg8 – h8

If White leaves his bishop on the a2–g8 diagonal — retreating it to b3, for example — then Black's king has no moves available and the game ends in **stalemate**. If the bishop vacates the a2–g8 diagonal, Black will simply move her king back and forth between g8 and h8.

But if the bishop were on e3 on the board shown left, White would have an easy win:

1.	h5 – h6 +	Kg7 – h8
2.	Kg5 – g6	Kh8 – g8
3.	Be3 – d4	

The black king cannot return to h8, as it would then be in check to the white bishop. The pawn can now advance to h8.

| 3. | . . . | Kg8 – f8 |
| 4. | h6 – h7 | |

In his next move White will **promote** the pawn to a queen and an easy win will follow.

To use a bishop to advantage in the type of ending discussed on the previous page, it must be on the same color square as the promotion square of the pawn. If White had been trying to promote a pawn on the a-file, instead of on the h-file, he would have needed a light-squared bishop.

Having a knight instead of a bishop to support the advance of a rook's pawn creates a different set of problems altogether, as the following games show.

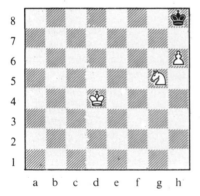

With the pieces in the position illustrated on the board above, the win is easy.

1. Kd4 – e5   Kh8 – g8
2. Ke5 – f6   Kg8 – h8
3. Kf6 – g6   Kh8 – g8
4. Ng5 – f7

The black king cannot return to the promotion square.

4. ...   Kg8 – f8
5. h6 – h7

And White can promote his

pawn on h8 with his next move.

This was a straightforward win, but in the next position (see the board below) the ending is drawn because the white knight is tied to the defense of the pawn on h7. If White moves his king up to protect the pawn, Black will be **stalemated**, as this next sequence shows.

1. Kd4 – e5   Kh8 – g7
2. Ke5 – f5   Kg7 – h8
3. Kf5 – g6 stalemate

And the game ends in a draw.

Remember!

King, bishop, and rook's pawn will draw against a lone king if the lone king reaches the promotion square. The exception is when the bishop is on the same color square as the promotion square, when a win will result.

116

▶ In this position, with a light-squared bishop opposing a dark-squared bishop, White has no control over the dark squares and won't be able to queen his extra pawns.

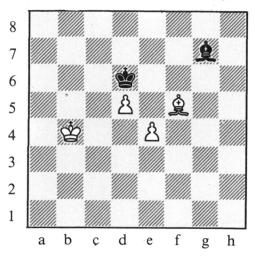

On the board above White cannot queen his extra pawns because his light-squared bishop is opposed by a dark-squared bishop. This type of ending is called "opposite-colored bishops," or "bishops of opposite color," and the name refers to the color of the squares on which the bishops stand and not to the color of the pieces.

The reason why this type of ending is so often drawn is that one side controls almost all the light squares, while the other controls nearly all the dark squares. Even though White is two pawns up in the position shown above, Black will capture the pawns if they advance. In order to draw, Black needs only to move her bishop backward and forward to safe squares along the a1–h8 diagonal. White cannot do anything — try it for yourself!

Pawn Majorities

The player who has the greater number of pawns on one side of the board is said to have a pawn majority on that flank. On the board below, for example, White has a queen's-side pawn majority (two to one) and Black has a king's-side pawn majority (four to three). A pawn majority often provides an opportunity to create a **passed pawn**, which can then be **promoted** to a queen.

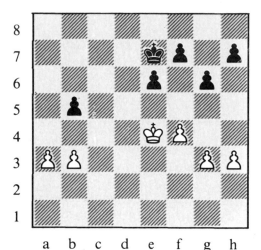

◄ White has a pawn majority on the queen's side in this position, while Black has one on the king's side.

On the board above, White can create a passed pawn immediately by playing a3–a4. If Black replies with . . . b5–b4, then the white a-pawn is passed and is free to queen, with the white king fending off any attack from the black king.

If Black captures instead, with . . . b5×a4, then White will recapture with b3×a4. This move will give White an outside passed pawn, or distant passed pawn — one that is distant from the defending king. The black king must speed to the queen's

side of the board to stop this pawn from queening. The white king will then attack the king's-side black pawns, since they are no longer defended by their king, and snatch as many of them as possible. For example:

1.	a3 – a4	b5 × a4
2.	b3 × a4	Ke7 – d6
3.	a4 – a5	Kd6 – c6
4.	a5 – a6	Kc6 – b6
5.	Ke4 – e5	Kb6 × a6
6.	Ke5 – f6	Ka6 – b6

The trap is set.

The black king now rushes

back across the board to the aid of its king's-side pawns, but it is too late.

7.	Kf6 × f7	Kb6 – c6
8.	Kf7 × e6	Kc6 – c5
9.	Ke6 – f6	Kc5 – d4
10.	Kf6 – g7	Kd4 – e4
11.	Kg7 × h7	Ke4 – f3
12.	Kh7 × g6	Kf3 × g3
13.	f4 – f5	

And Black cannot prevent the white f-pawn from queening on the f8 square.

This example shows how useful an outside passed pawn can be as a decoy, in distracting the defending king from its duty to its own pawns.

Not all pawn majorities will produce a passed pawn. On the board below, for instance, White has a queen's-side pawn majority, but his b-pawns are **doubled** and this will stop him from creating a passed pawn.

Black, on the other hand, can exploit her extra king's-side pawn in order to divert the attention of the white king. The following moves might be made in this game.

1.	. . .	h7 – h5
2.	a3 – a4	g5 – g4

Black must not play 2. . . . b5 × a4, because White could then reply with the move b3 × a4, thereby resolving his doubled pawns.

3.	h3 × g4	h5 × g4
4.	a4 – a5	g4 – g3
5.	Ke3 – f3	Ke5 – d4
6.	Kf3 × g3	Kd4 – c3
7.	Kg3 – f3	Kc3 × b4
8.	Kf3 – e3	Kb4 × b3
9.	Ke3 – d3	b5 – b4
10.	Kd3 – d2	Kb3 – a2

Now Black controls the b1 square, where her b-pawn will queen in three moves.

▶ **Although White has** a queen's-side pawn majority here, his doubled pawns on the b-file will prevent him from creating a passed pawn.

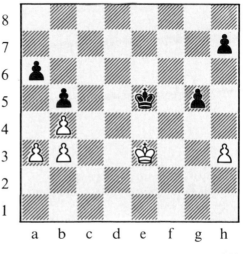

Rook-and-pawn Endings

This is the most common type of ending in chess. Rook-and-pawn endings are difficult to play and whole books have been written about the techniques necessary.

The ending of king, rook, and pawn against king and rook is most often drawn if the defending king controls the pawn's queening square and is usually a loss if it doesn't.

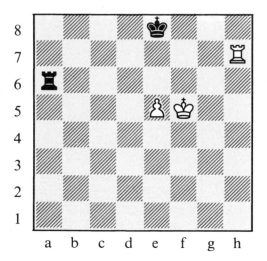

◄ **The black king** controls the queening square here, so Black should be able to force a draw.

If White were to open with the rook move Rh7–h8+, with the pieces in the position illustrated above, he would not be able to drive the black king away from the e8 square — Black would simply play . . . Ke8–e7. So White will try to advance his pawn instead.

1. e5 – e6

Black's best strategy here is to attack from behind.

1. . . .   Ra6 – a1
2. Kf5 – f6   Ra1 – f1+

3. Kf6 – e5   Rf1 – e1+
4. Ke5 – d6   Re1 – d1+
5. Kd6 – e5   Rd1 – e1+

A draw by repetition of position is looming (see page 108). White's only way of avoiding this is to move his king back to the 2nd rank, but this will leave his pawn unprotected.

6. Ke5 – f5   Re1 – f1+
7. Kf5 – g4   Rf1 – g1+
8. Kg4 – f3   Rg1 – e1

The black rook is now attacking the white pawn. White moves

120

his rook to h6 to protect it.

9.   Rh7 – h6   Ke8 – e7

Black renews her assault on the white pawn and will capture it with the rook on her next move.

Note that before White's first move, advancing his pawn to the e6 square, Black's defensive rook is best stationed on the 6th rank (a6 or b6) to prevent the white king from advancing.

The next example illustrates what happens when the defending king cannot control the queening square. This is the famous Lucena position, named after a 15th-century Spaniard who was the author of the earliest surviving printed work on chess.

On the board below, the white king controls the e8 square. Even so, Black may be able to force a draw if she can either keep the white king on e8 or harass it with constant rook checks if it moves off the all-important queening square. White will therefore have to provide a shelter for his king and this is how he does it.

1.	Rd1 – d4	Rf2 – f1
2.	Rd4 – c4 +	Kc8 – b7
3.	Ke8 – d7	Rf1 – d1 +
4.	Kd7 – e6	Rd1 – e1 +
5.	Ke6 – d6	Re1 – d1 +
6.	Kd6 – e5	Rd1 – e1 +
7.	Rc4 – d4	

Black has run out of checks, and White will now be able to **promote** his pawn. This is one of the most common ways to win this type of ending.

It was essential for White to place his rook on d4 before moving his king, as without this precaution Black could have gone on checking forever. This most complicated operation is often called "building a bridge."

▶ **In this position the** white king controls the queening square, so Black will find it difficult to avoid losing the game.

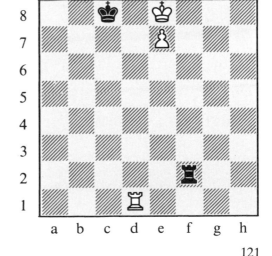

The Square of the Pawn

In the endgame it is important to know whether the enemy king can catch a **passed pawn** in time to prevent it from queening. This simple test will help you to work out whether your opponent's king is a threat to your passed pawn.

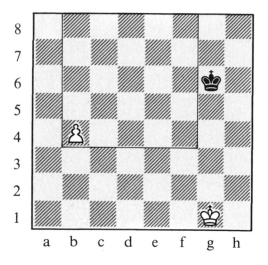

◀ **In this position the** black king can penetrate the square of the pawn on its next move. White won't be able to queen his pawn.

Draw a large imaginary square on the chessboard, taking the queening square as one corner and the square currently occupied by the pawn as another, as on the board above. If the enemy king can move inside this square before your pawn next advances, it will be able to reach the queening square in time to block your pawn's promotion. If the king is too far away, your pawn will be able to rush forward to queen in safety.

Simple Checkmates

If you have a queen on the board, or have been lucky enough to queen a pawn, then it is important to know how to use your extra **material** to **checkmate** your opponent. Five simple checkmating positions are outlined in the next few pages.

The following are known to be wins for the side with the extra material: king and queen against king; king and rook against king;

king and two bishops against king; and king, bishop, and knight against king. With these combinations of pieces, on the other hand, the endings will be drawn: king and two knights against king; king and bishop, against king; and king and knight against king. The ending king and two knights against king can be lost by very careless play, but it is impossible to lose with either a king and knight or a king and bishop against a **lone king**.

King and queen against king

On the board below left, White's strategy should be to force Black's king into a corner or to the edge of the board. The easiest way to learn this ending is to use only your queen until you have forced the enemy king into a rectangle measuring three squares by one square, at the edge of the board (see the board below right).

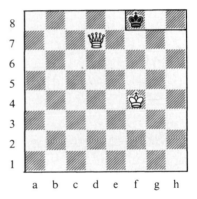

It is White's turn to move.

1.	Qf1 – b5	Kd6 – e6
2.	Qb5 – c5	Ke6 – f6
3.	Qc5 – e5 +	Kf6 – f7
4.	Qe5 – d6	Kf7 – g7
5.	Qd6 – e6	Kg7 – f8
6.	Qe6 – d7	

Black's king is now contained within the rectangle of f8, g8, and h8 (see the board above right). If White's queen remains

on d7, Black's king cannot move outside these three squares, as to do so would place it in check.

| 6. | . . . | Kf8 – g8 |

White now brings up his king to support the queen.

7.	Kf4 – f5	Kg8 – f8
8.	Kf5 – f6	Kf8 – g8
9.	Qd7 – g7 checkmate	

White has won the game.

King and rook against king

Winning with a king and a rook takes a little longer than with a king and a queen, but the strategy is still very straightforward — the lone king must be driven to the edge of the board. The reason that this play takes longer is that the lone king can attack the rook, whereas a king can never attack a queen.

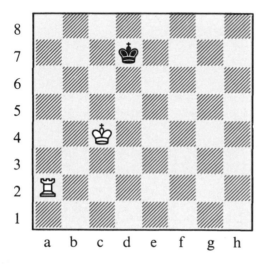

◀ **With the pieces in** this position, White should be able to force the black king to the 8th rank and hold it there until his rook can checkmate it.

The first stage of the strategy is to decide on which edge of the board the lone king will be checkmated. The king should then be restrained as near to that edge as possible.

On the board illustrated above, the nearest edge to the black king is the 8th rank. At the moment the king is on the 7th rank, and it should therefore be prevented from getting closer to the center of the board.

1.   Ra2 – a6

This move restricts the black king to the 7th and 8th ranks, as

moving to the 6th rank would place it in check to the rook. If the white rook remains on the 6th rank, the black king will be unable to cross the barrier White has created. When playing this ending, don't block the white rook's action by moving your king across the 6th rank, as this would allow Black's king to escape into the open.

1.   . . .   Kd7 – e7

The next stage of White's plan is to bring his king nearer to the black king, but *not* to gain the **opposition**. In this game neither player wants the opposition.

2.   Kc4 – d5   Ke7 – f7

If Black plays 2. . . . Ke7 – d7 instead, she will gain the opposition, but White can then force the lone king to the edge of the board immediately, with 3. Ra6 – a7+. That's why in this situation it is a disadvantage to have the opposition.

3.   Kd5 – e5   Kf7 – g7

The move 3. . . . Kf7–e7 would let White force Black's king to the edge, with 4. Ra6–a7+

4.   Ke5 – f5   Kg7 – h7
5.   Kf5 – g5   Kh7 – g7

Black must either take the opposition at this point (which she doesn't want to do), or retreat at once.

6.   Ra6 – a7+   Kg7 – f8

The board below shows the position after Black's sixth move. The black king has been forced to the edge of the board, so the white king can now close in for the kill.

7.   Kg5 – g6   Kf8 – e8

If Black takes the opposition instead here, she will be checkmated next move: 7. . . . Kf8 –g8 would be met by 8. Ra7–a8 checkmate.

8.   Kg6 – f6   Ke8 – d8
9.   Kf6 – e6   Kd8 – c8
10. Ke6 – d6   Kc8 – b8

Now the rook is under attack and must move, but the black king is nearing the end of the road.

11. Ra7 – c7   Kb8 – a8
12. Kd6 – c6   Ka8 – b8
13. Kc6 – b6   Kb8 – a8
14. Rc7 – c8 checkmate

White has won the game.

▶ **The black king has** been forced to the edge of the board. White must now trap it in one corner so that his rook can checkmate it.

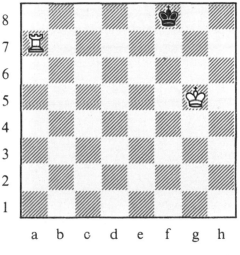

King and two bishops against king

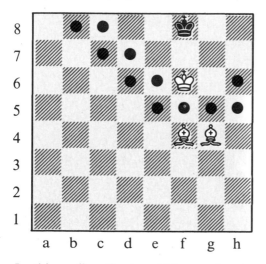

◄ **The first stage of** this ending is to use the two bishops to contain the enemy king within two impenetrable "walls," indicated here by dots.

In this ending the two bishops are brought to adjacent squares so that they contain the lone king within two impenetrable "walls." On the board above, there is one wall two diagonals thick stretching from f4 and g4 to b8 and c8, and another shorter wall from f4 and g4 to h6 and h5. These restrict Black's king to the right-hand corner.

The winning technique lies in driving the lone king into its nearest corner, without allow-ing it to break through either wall.

1. Bg4 – d7

White forces the black king to-ward the h8 corner.

1.	. . .	Kf8 – g8
2.	Kf6 – g6	Kg8 – f8
3.	Bf4 – d6 +	Kf8 – g8
4.	Bd7 – e6 +	Kg8 – h8
5.	Bd6 – e5 checkmate	

Black's king is trapped and White has won the game.

King, bishop, and knight against king

This ending is much more complex than the previous ones. The position given here is an easy example, but it can take as many as 34 moves, with skillful play by both sides, to drive the lone king into the correct corner and deliver checkmate.

Positioning the enemy king in the correct corner is very important in this ending. On the board illustrated below, the white bishop is operating along the dark squares and it is vital that the lone king is forced into the dark corner — the h8 square. With a light-squared bishop, the enemy king must be driven into the light corner.

The winning strategy has two to three stages. First of all the lone king is forced toward an edge of the board. Next it must be driven toward a corner. It is often necessary to direct the king to the "wrong" corner — one that is the wrong color — before it is possible to coordinate the attacking pieces in the best way. Finally, the lone king is forced along the edge of the board, from the "wrong" corner to the correct one.

Don't resign if you reach this ending and find yourself with the lone king. Your opponent might not know how to force checkmate within 50 moves and you may be able to draw the game under the 50-move rule (see page 107).

On the board below, it is White's turn to move. Set up your own chessboard and follow the sequence.

| 1. | Kg4 – f5 | Kg7 – h7 |

If Black plays . . . Kg7–g8 instead, the move will be followed by 2. Kf5–g6 Kg8–h8, 3. Ne5 –g4 Kh8–g8, 4. Ng4–h6+ Kg8 –h8 and 5. Be7–f6 checkmate.

2.	Be7 – f8	Kh7 – g8
3.	Bf8 – h6	Kg8 – h7
4.	Ne5 – g4	Kh7 – g8
5.	Kg5 – g6	Kg8 – h8
6.	Bh6 – g7 +	Kh8 – g8
7.	Ng4 – h6 checkmate

White has won the game.

▶ **This ending** position is difficult to play, but by moving his pieces skillfully White should be able to deliver checkmate.

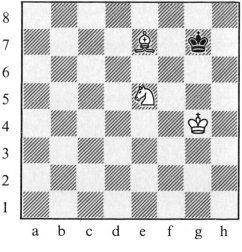

King and two knights against king

This ending should always be a draw, because the player with the king and two knights can deliver checkmate only if the opposing side plays badly. Checkmating positions like the one above are the result of poor defense on the part of the player with the lone king.

The following moves illus-

trate what happens if Black defends sensibly, even though her king is already in the corner (see the board below).

1. Kf5 – g6   Kh8 – g8
2. Ne5 – d7

White moves to prevent the black king from coming nearer to the center, with the move 2. . . . Kg8–f8.

2. . . .   Kg8 – h8
3. Nd6 – e8   Kh8 – g8
4. Ne8 – f6+   Kg8 – h8

Any move by the white knight on d7 will now produce a **stalemate** (see pages 61–63). The same will apply if White plays Kg6–h6 on his fifth move. And if White plays anything else, Black will carry on moving her king as before.

◄ **Although her king** is already in the corner, with sensible play Black should be able to force a draw from this position.

7: Chess Champions

This chapter looks at the careers and sporting styles of the greatest chess players of all time, the world champions. One of the best ways for you to improve your strength at the chessboard is by studying the games of the most distinguished proponents of the art of chess. Each champion has their own particular brand of play — be it aggressive, attacking, tactical, or strategic — which is just as personal as their signature.

Try to identify which champion's games appeal most to you and then study them in depth. This will provide you with a systematic method of playing. The "adopt a hero" technique has worked well for many chess experts, including World Champion Gary Kasparov (above), whose personal chess hero is Alexander Alekhine.

The Early Champions

The first officially recognized world chess championship was held in 1886, when Wilhelm Steinitz beat Johannes Zukertort in a match held in the United States. The outstanding players before that date are known, but there was no official champion.

The Spaniard Ruy Lopez (*c.* 1530–80) achieved his reputation by beating the best Italian players and by writing the *Libro del Axedrez*, a collection of chess openings and general advice and analysis. The leading Italian players at this time were Paolo Boi (1528–98) and Leonardo da Cutri (1542–87). Boi was renowned for his ability to play three games at once without sight of the board (**blindfold chess**), a skill that astonished his contemporaries. Leonardo was Boi's greatest rival and was considered his equal in playing strength.

A generation later, Giaochino Greco (1600–34) was the best-known Italian master. He traveled throughout Europe playing matches for high stakes and compiled manuscripts on chess openings, two of which survive in the Bodleian Library in Oxford and the British Library in London. Many of Greco's games were written down and later published. Here is one of those games, played against an unknown opponent.

Greco is White in this game.

| 1. | e2 – e4 | b7 – b6 |
| 2. | d2 – d4 | Bc8 – b7 |

This setup by Black has had a revival in popularity during the last two decades.

| 3. | Bf1 – d3 | f7 – f5 |
| 4. | e4 × f5 | Bb7 × g2 |

Black's move appears strong, but it allows an early attack against her king.

5.	Qd1 – h5 +	g7 – g6
6.	f5 × g6	Ng8 – f6
7.	g6 × h7 +	Nf6 × h5
8.	Bd3 – g6 checkmate	

An easy win for Greco.

After Spain and Italy it was the turn of France to produce the world's greatest chess players. François-André Danican Philidor (1726–95), the musician and composer, dominated French and English chess circles for nearly half a century. He was the first player to try to systematize chess knowledge and his *Analyse du Jeu des Echecs* is a famous analysis of the game. Philidor was the first great player to understand the importance of pawns, which he described as "the soul of chess." He is also remembered for the defense 1. e2–e4 e7–e5, 2. Ng1–f3 d7–d6, which is named after him.

Philidor's mantle as the world's leading player was taken over by another Frenchman, Alexandre Deschapelles (1780–1847), who fought for Napoleon and lost his right hand in battle. Despite this handicap he successfully played billiards, pushing the cue with his stump. He also fought numerous duels with his good left hand and was an accomplished bridge player (he invented the Deschapelles coup). An extremely talented chess player, Deschapelles was also amazingly boastful and claimed that he had learned all his skill at chess in two days.

Deschapelles's pupil, Louis

▲ The 18th-century's leading player, Philidor was a master of blindfold chess. This engraving depicts him playing blindfold at Parsloe's Club in London on February 23, 1784, in the presence of the Turkish ambassador.

La Bourdonnais (1797–1840), was the next player to be regarded as the unofficial world champion. In 1834 he defeated the leading Irish player Alexander McDonnell in a marathon series of matches that involved 85 individual games. La Bourdonnais won 45 games and lost 27, with 13 draws.

By 1843 Howard Staunton (1810–74) had become Europe's

131

leading player. Howard Staunton is the only British player ever to have been recognized as the world's greatest master. In 1841 he founded the first successful chess magazine in England, the *Chess Player's Chronicle*. He was also the author of a chess column in the *Illustrated London News*, which he frequently used to attack other leading chess players and writers of the day. Staunton was a noted Shakespearean scholar and his three-volume edition of the plays first appeared in 1857. His two great contributions to chess literature were the books *Chess Praxis* and *The Chess Player's Handbook*.

Staunton's two great rivals during his lifetime were the American genius Paul Morphy (1837–84), and Adolf Anderssen (1818–78) of Germany. Morphy challenged Staunton to a match in 1858 but was refused. Staunton claimed at the time that he was too busy, but cowardice is more likely to have been the reason.

When Morphy arrived in Europe in 1858 it was clear from the quality of his games that he had already outstripped Anderssen and Staunton. After Staunton refused his challenge, Morphy played a match with

◀ **Although one of the 19th** century's most brilliant chess players, the American Paul Morphy played fewer than 75 serious games.

Anderssen and won easily. But a few months later Morphy retired from serious play and, for the remainder of his life, was something of a recluse.

Also in 1858, Morphy played chess against the Duke of Brunswick and Count Isouard de Vauvenargue in Paris. The game took place in the duke's box at the opera during a performance of Bellini's *Norma*. The board below shows the position after Black's ninth move. Morphy is White.

10.	Nc3 × b5	c6 × b5
11.	Bc4 × b5+	Nb8 – d7
12.	0–0–0	

The white queen's rook occupies the open d-file. Morphy is now threatening to play 13. Rd1 × d7. After this move, whatever Black does in reply, the black queen will be lost.

12.	...	Ra8 – d8
13.	Rd1 × d7!	Rd8 × d7
14.	Rh1 – d1	

Morphy brings his remaining

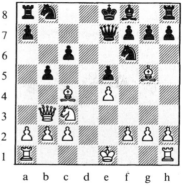

▲ **The German Adolf Anderssen**
was one of the world's most
successful tournament players.

undeveloped piece into play and
renews the pressure on the d7
square.

14. . . .   Qe7 – e6

Now Morphy unleashes his
checkmating attack.

15. Bb5 × d7 +   Nf6 × d7
16. Qb3 – b8 + !!   Nd7 × b8
17. Rd1 – d8 checkmate

And that is how Morphy won
the famous game in Paris against
the aristocratic duo.

Paul Morphy's contempo-
rary, Adolf Anderssen, was the
last of the unofficial world chess
champions. His primary claim
to fame stems from his victory at
the London chess tournament of
1851, which is widely regarded
as the first international tournament although one or two had
been held before this date.

Anderssen's best games include two that are considered to
this day to be among the most
brilliant games of all time. They
are known as the Immortal and
the Evergreen.

The Immortal game

This was played in London on the occasion of, but not within, the famous 1851 tournament. Anderssen's opponent, Lionel Kieseritsky, was born in Livonia and later settled in Paris. He originated the Kieseritsky variation of the King's Gambit, which was an extremely popular opening during the mid to late 19th century.

In this game, Anderssen is White and Kieseritsky, Black. It is known as the King's Bishop's Gambit.

1.	e2 – e4	e7 – e5
2.	f2 – f4	e5 × f4
3.	Bf1 – c4	Qd8 – h4 +
4.	Ke1 – f1	b7 – b5?!
5.	Bc4 × b5	Ng8 – f6
6.	Ng1 – f3	Qh4 – h6
7.	d2 – d3	Nf6 – h5
8.	Nf3 – h4!	Qh6 – g5
9.	Nh4 – f5	c7 – c6?

The board below shows the position after Kieseritsky's ninth move in this game.

10.	Rh1 – g1!!	c6 × b5
11.	g2 – g4	Nh5 – f6
12.	h2 – h4	Qg5 – g6
13.	h4 – h5	Qg6 – g5
14.	Qd1 – f3	Nf6 – g8
15.	Bc1 × f4	Qg5 – f6

▶ **The position after Black's** ninth move in the 1851 game between Anderssen (White) and Kieseritsky (Black).

16.	Nb1 – c3	Bf8 – c5
17.	Nc3 – d5!	

In the final stage of the game, Anderssen offers a pawn and then two rooks in order to gain time for his attack. Kieseritsky accepts the sacrifice but soon finds that Anderssen's most important remaining pieces are in play, while his own defenses are a shambles.

17.	. . .	Qf6 × b2
18.	Bf4 – d6!	Qb2 × a1 +
19.	Kf1 – e2	Bc5 × g1
20.	e4 – e5!	Nb8 – a6?
21.	Nf5 × g7 +	Ke8 – d8
22.	Qf3 – f6 + !	Ng8 × f6
23.	Bd6 – e7 checkmate	

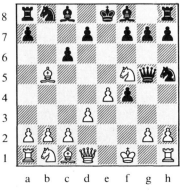

135

The Evergreen game

The second of Anderssen's most brilliant games was played in Berlin in 1852. Anderssen's opponent, Jean Dufresne, was actually a German player and writer whose real name was E. S. Freund.

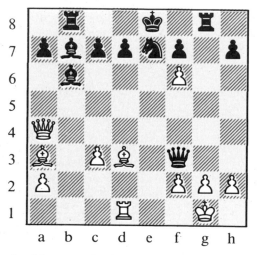

◀ **The position of the** pieces after Black's 20th move in the famous Evergreen game. Anderssen played White.

In this game Anderssen is again White, while Black is played by Dufresne. The opening is called Evans Gambit.

1.	e2 – e4	e7 – e5
2.	Ng1 – f3	Nb8 – c6
3.	Bf1 – c4	Bf8 – c5
4.	b2 – b4	Bc5 × b4
5.	c2 – c3	Bb4 – a5
6.	d2 – d4	e5 × d4
7.	0–0	d4 – d3?!
8.	Qd1 – b3	Qd8 – f6
9.	e4 – e5	Qf6 – g6
10.	Rf1 – e1	Ng8 – e7
11.	Bc1 – a3	b7 – b5
12.	Qb3 × b5	Ra8 – b8
13.	Qb5 – a4	Ba5 – b6
14.	Nb1 – d2	Bc8 – b7?

15.	Nd2 – e4	Qg6 – f5?
16.	Bc4 × d3	Qf5 – h5
17.	Ne4 – f6 + !	g7 × f6
18.	e5 × f6	Rh8 – g8
19.	Ra1 – d1	Qh5 × f3?
20.	Re1 × e7 + !	Nc6 × e7
21.	Qa4 × d7 + !!	Ke8 × d7
22.	Bd3 – f5 +	Kd7 – e8
23.	Bf5 – d7 +	Ke8 – f8
24.	Ba3 × e7 checkmate

The diagram above illustrates the position after Dufresne's 20th move.

The great coincidence here is that, as in the Immortal, Anderssen delivers checkmate with a bishop on the e7 square. Both games will repay close study.

The Modern Champions

1886–1894	Wilhelm Steinitz	Austria
1894–1921	Emanuel Lasker	Germany
1921–1927	José Capablanca	Cuba
1927–1935	Alexander Alekhine	U.S.S.R. & France
1935–1937	Max Euwe	Netherlands
1937–1946	Alexander Alekhine	
1948–1957	Mikhail Botvinnik	U.S.S.R.
1957–1958	Vassily Smyslov	U.S.S.R.
1958–1960	Mikhail Botvinnik	
1960–1961	Mikhail Tal	U.S.S.R.
1961–1963	Mikhail Botvinnik	
1963–1969	Tigran Petrosian	U.S.S.R.
1969–1972	Boris Spassky	U.S.S.R.
1972–1975	Bobby Fischer	U.S.A.
1975–1985	Anatoly Karpov	U.S.S.R.
1985–	Gary Kasparov	U.S.S.R.

▲ **In 1886 Wilhelm Steinitz** became the first official world chess champion.

Wilhelm Steinitz (1836–1900)

Steinitz was born in Prague and studied in Vienna. His unofficial reign as world champion can be dated from 1866 when he defeated Adolf Anderssen, who was at that time regarded as the best player in the world. But it was only in 1886 that Steinitz felt able to call himself "world chess champion" without contradiction, after he defeated his greatest rival, Johannes Zukertort.

His influence on modern chess theory was immense. Steinitz understood the importance of building up positional advantages in order to win, and his ideas were published in his book *Modern Chess Theory* in 1889. In 1894 Steinitz lost the world championship title to the rising star Emanuel Lasker. His final years were troubled with mental illness and he died penniless in New York, where he was buried in Evergreen Cemetery, Brooklyn.

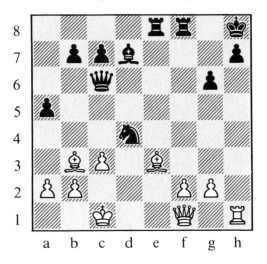

◄ **The position after** Black's 23rd move in the 1892 world championship match. Steinitz played White and Tchigorin was Black.

The position above arose after Black's 23rd move in a game played during the 1892 world championship match in Havana, Cuba. Steinitz concluded the game with an original mating attack along the h-file.

In this game, White is Steinitz and Black is Mikhail Tchigorin, a Russian chess player.

24. Rh1 × h7 + !!	Kh8 × h7
25. Qf1 – h1 +	Kh7 – g7
26. Be3 – h6 +	Kg7 – f6
27. Qh1 – h4 +	Kf6 – e5
28. Qh4 – d4 +	Ke5 – f5
29. Qd4 – f4 checkmate	

And Steinitz wins the game.

Emanuel Lasker (1868–1941)

Holding the title for a record 27 years (1894–1921), and defending it regularly against powerful opponents, Lasker has claims to being the greatest ever world champion. He also won almost every first-class tournament that he entered during his long reign.

Lasker's greatest strength lay in the middle game, where he created amazing complications. Any opponents who survived that phase of the game were worn down in the endgame. As White, Lasker preferred to play the Exchange variation of the Ruy Lopez opening: 1. e2–e4 e7–e5; 2. Ng1–f3 Nb3–c6; 3. Bf1–b5 a7–a6; 4. Bb5×c6 (see also pages 69–71). As Black, he

▲ **The German player Emanuel** Lasker held the title of world champion for a record 27 years.

favored the Orthodox defense to the Queen's Gambit: 1. d2 –d4 d7–d5; 2. c2–c4 e7–e6; 3. Nb1–c3 Ng8–f6; 4. Bc1–g5 Bf8 –e7 (see also pages 82–84).

Lasker was a great chess teacher, and his publications included *Common Sense in Chess* and *Lasker's Chess Manual.* He was one of the first players to employ psychology in his games, attempting moves that may not have been the strongest choice objectively, but which he felt were unpleasant for a particular opponent.

José Capablanca (1888–1942)

A Cuban with a great natural talent, Capablanca learned chess at the age of four by watching his father playing with a friend. On the third day of this game, young José noticed his father moving a knight from one light square to another. Afterward he told his father that he had cheated, and when his father complained that the boy did not know how to play, José promptly challenged him and beat him twice!

After studying in the United States, Capablanca entered the Cuban Foreign Office as a commercial attaché. This allowed him to travel abroad, and in

▲ **José Capablanca in 1919,** two years before he won the world title from Emanuel Lasker.

1919 he won the international tournament at Hastings, England. Two years later he took the world championship title from Lasker without losing a single game during the match, a feat that gave him the reputation of being unbeatable. His best-known books are *My Chess Career* and *Chess Fundamentals*.

Capablanca's hallmark was his liking for clear, simple positions. If you study some of his games, you'll be surprised at how easy they look.

Alexander Alekhine (1892–1946)

Alekhine was born in Moscow and was taught chess by his mother. The game soon became the great passion of his life, and in his boyhood he played **correspondence chess** avidly. He started to play in tournaments in his teens and came in third in the St. Petersburg tournament of 1914. He won the first Soviet Championship in 1920 and in the following year emigrated to Switzerland, later settling in Paris.

Once in Paris, Alekhine began preparing to challenge Capablanca for the world title. He studied chess for eight hours daily and wrote what is regarded as his most important work, *My Best Games of Chess 1908–23*. A second volume, *My Best Games of Chess 1924–37*, was published later.

In those days, there was no accepted set of regulations governing world championship matches, and the reigning champion could make almost any stipulation he wished. When Capablanca held the title he insisted that any challenger should put up a stake of $10,000 in gold. Naturally, this dissuaded most **grandmasters**, but in 1927

▼ Alekhine playing blindfold chess in Paris, against 28 of the most famous French players. He won 22 and drew three, losing only three games.

Alekhine found some backers for his quest for the title. He defeated Capablanca in that year in a match that developed into a war of attrition, with Alekhine scoring six wins, three losses and no less than 25 draws.

Alekhine successfully defended his title against Bogoljubow in 1929 and 1934, but in 1935 he was beaten by the Dutchman Max Euwe, who held the title for two years before Alekhine won it back again. This two-year lapse was generally regarded as having more to do with Alekhine's fondness for alcohol than with Euwe's superiority as a player. After regaining the title in 1937, Alekhine kept it until his death nine years later.

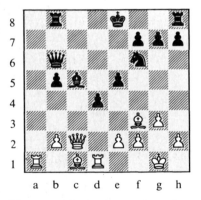

The position above is taken from one of Alekhine's most brilliant middle games. Alekhine was White and his opponent was Klaus Junge, a promising German player who died in 1945 at age twenty-one.

The game was played in Prague in 1942 and the board shows the position after Junge's 17th move.

18. Ra1 – a6!!

A magnificent and unexpected rook sacrifice. At the expense of exchanging rook for bishop, Alekhine hopes to trap the black king in the middle of the board.

18. . . .	Qb6 × a6
19. Qc2 × c5	Qa6 – e6
20. Bf3 – c6 +	Nf6 – d7
21. Bc6 × d7 +	Ke8 × d7
22. Qc5 – a7 +	Kd7 – c6

If Junge plays 22. . . . Kd7–c8 instead, then 23. Bc1–d2 followed by Rd1–c1 will prove decisive.

| 23. Bc1 – d2 | Rh8 – c8 |
| 24. e2 – e4 | Qe6 – b3 |

Alekhine was threatening 25. Rd1–c1 + Kc6–d6, 26. Bd2–b4 +. Note how the white queen and rook now work together to hunt down the black king.

25. Rd1 – a1	b5 – b4
26. Ra1 – a6 +	Kc6 – b5
27. Ra6 – a5 +	Kb5 – c6
28. Qa7 – c5 +	Kc6 – d7
29. Ra5 – a7 +	Black resigns

The black king cannot escape the checkmating net. If Junge plays 29. . . . Kd7–e6, then 30. Qc5–e7 delivers checkmate. If he plays 29. . . . Kd7–d8 instead, then 30. Qc5–e7 will end the game in the same way.

Max Euwe (1901–1981)

Euwe was taught to play chess at the age of four by his mother and entered his first tournament when he was ten. He scored well in international tournaments and matches, but his win against Alekhine in 1935 was unexpected and he was unable to retain the title in the revenge match two years later.

Euwe was a mathematician as well as a chess player and divided his time between teaching and chess. In his later years he became an expert in computer-based information sciences. In 1970 he turned to chess adminis-tration when he was elected president of **FIDE**.

Euwe was a prolific chess writer. Among his most famous works are *Judgement and Planning in Chess*, *The Middle Game* (with Kramer), and *The Road to Chess Mastery* (with Meiden). His playing style was solid and scientific, and he was responsible for systematizing openings study through his series *Chess Opening Theory*.

▼ **Max Euwe (right) had a brief** two years as world champion. He is playing Capablanca here.

Mikhail Botvinnik (1911–   )

Botvinnik was the first Soviet chess player to win the world championship (Alekhine had adopted French nationality before his defeat of Capablanca), holding the title in 1948–57, 1958–60, and 1961–63. During his years of supremacy the U.S.S.R. became the leading chess nation of the world. From 1948 until the present day all of the world champions, with the exception of Fischer, have been Soviet citizens.

Botvinnik's chess talent was noticed at an early age, and in 1925 he played against Capablanca when the Cuban gave a **simultaneous exhibition** in Moscow. Botvinnik rose to prominence in 1931, when he won the U.S.S.R. championship, and in 1936 he was hailed as a national hero after sharing first place with Capablanca at the Nottingham tournament in England.

In 1946 the death of Alekhine left the world championship vacant, and Botvinnik was the favorite to take the crown. For

▼ **Botvinnik in March 1963,** during the third game of the match in which he lost his title to Tigran Petrosian.

the first time since its foundation in 1924 **FIDE** was involved in the organization of a world championship competition and four **grandmasters** were selected to compete with Botvinnik for the title. In 1948 the five contenders played each other five times in a match-tournament, which Botvinnik won in overwhelming style, finishing three points ahead of Smyslov, his nearest rival.

Smyslov dethroned Botvinnik briefly in 1957. As ex-champion Botvinnik had the right to demand a return match, and when this took place the following year Botvinnik regained the title. In 1960 Botvinnik again lost a championship match, this time to Tal, but won it back a year later in the return match. He once told me that when you are world champion you treat the title as though you own it, and you cannot believe that it might fall into the hands of someone else.

Botvinnik surrendered the title for the last time in 1963, to Petrosian, and seven years later announced his retirement from active play. He set up a chess school whose most famous graduate, Gary Kasparov, became the youngest ever world champion when he won the title in 1985 at the age of 22.

Part of the secret of Botvinnik's genius is his capacity for hard work. At the end of each game he analyzes his play in-

tensively. He was also the first player to suggest that chess preparation or training should include physical as well as mental exercise. Many people think of chess purely as a game that involves mental energy, but in a long and arduous chess tournament or match the players often become physically exhausted as well.

Botvinnik's most instructive chess book is *One Hundred Selected Games 1926–46*. He has also written extensively about computer chess, a subject to which he has devoted much of his time since the late 1960s.

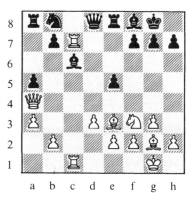

The position above is from a game between Botvinnik and the Hungarian grandmaster, Lajos Portisch. It was played in Monaco in 1968 and Botvinnik was White and Portisch, Black.

Botvinnik has won a pawn but in doing so he has allowed his rook to become trapped on c7. The rook is now under threat from the black queen. However, Botvinnik envisaged this several moves ago and has worked out a winning plan.

17. Rc1 × c6

By eliminating the black queen's bishop, Botvinnik gains control of the central light squares, enabling his bishop on g2 to come into play later with good effect.

17. ...   b7 × c6
18. Rc7 × f7!!

Botvinnik now unleashes an impressive rook **sacrifice**.

18. ...   h7 – h6

Botvinnik's plan is based on Portisch capturing the rook. If Portisch had done this, his king would have fallen quickly: 18. . . . Kg8×f7; 19. Qa4–c4+ Kf7–g6; 20. Qc4–g4+ Kg6–f7; 21. Nf3–g5+ Kf7–g8; 22. Qg4 –c4+ Kg8–h8; 23. Ng5–f7+ Kh8–g8; 24. Nf7–h6++ (**double check**); then 24. . . . Kg8–h8 and 25. Qc4–g8 checkmate.

But Portisch's last move (18. . . . h7–h6) prevents the white knight from coming to g5 in this variation. So Botvinnik must first remove his rook from the immediate threat of capture.

19. Rf7 – b7	Qd8 – c8
20. Qa4 – c4+	Kg8 – h8
21. Nf3 – h4!!	Qc8 × b7
22. Nh4 – g6+	Kh8 – h7
23. Bg2 – e4	Bf8 – d6
24. Ng6 × e5 +	

This is an example of a **discov-** ered check. The white knight has moved away from the b1–h7 diagonal, leaving the black king in check to the white e4 bishop.

24. ...	g7 – g6
25. Be4 × g6+	Kh7 – g7
26. Be3 × h6+!!	Black resigns

Portisch resigns because 26. . . . Kg7×h6 would be followed by 27. Qc4–h4+ Kh6–g7, 28. Qh4 –h7+ Kg7–f6, 29. Ne5–g4+ Kf6–e6, and 30. Qh7×b7. Botvinnik would capture the black queen on his 30th move and an easy win for him would follow.

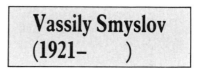

Vassily Smyslov (1921–   )

Smyslov was world champion in 1957–58 and was the first player to defeat Botvinnik in a title match. He was born in Moscow and was taught chess by his father who was a strong player. He first achieved fame in 1945, when he twice defeated the American **grandmaster** Samuel Reshevsky, in a match between the U.S.S.R. and the U.S. that was played via radio (each team was in its own country).

Smyslov was selected to play in the 1948 world championship match-tournament and came second. In 1954 he played Botvinnik for the world title, but the match was drawn and Botvinnik remained world champion.

Three years later Smyslov had another chance and this time he defeated Botvinnik. But Smyslov held the title only briefly, losing it a year later in the revenge match.

Smyslov has had an amazingly successful career as a **candidate** in the world championship cycle. He reached the final eliminating stage of the competition (the candidates' stage) in 1959, 1964, and 1982 but didn't succeed in qualifying to play another title match. Even so, in his sixties he is still a very powerful opponent in a field where most of the leading contenders are not much over 35 years old.

Smyslov has an outstanding tournament record and is regarded as an expert on endgame theory. He has written an autobiography and a collection of games entitled *My Best Games of Chess 1935–57*. A fine baritone, in his spare time he enjoys singing opera.

▼ **World champion for just one** year, 1957–58, Smyslov nevertheless has an outstanding tournament record and is an expert on endgame theory.

Mikhail Tal (1936–   )

Tal first won international acclaim in 1958, when he took first place in the **interzonal** tournament at Portorož, Yugoslavia, an event that was to launch him on the road to the world title. Two years later he had earned the right to challenge Botvinnik for the crown, and in 1960 he became the youngest world champion in the history of the game. The following year he lost the return match to Botvinnik, and since then his attempts to regain the title have been hampered by ill health.

Tal is noted for the genius of his attacking style. He plays for wild sacrificial complications in the middle game, picking moves that are not necessarily the best, but which he feels will most confuse his opponent. He is widely respected as a chess journalist and is the author of the classic works *Tal–Botvinnik — Match for the World Championship* (about the 1960 match) and *The Life and Games of Mikhail Tal*.

▼ Probably the greatest attacking genius of modern chess, Mikhail Tal was world champion from 1960 to 1961.

Tigran Petrosian (1929–1984)

Petrosian was born in Tbilisi, the capital of Soviet Georgia. He was taught checkers and backgammon by his parents when he was only four, and he believed that these games helped him to learn chess a few years later. He played in numerous junior events in the U.S.S.R. and by 1953 had established himself as one of the world's top players. But the strength of competition at the highest levels of international chess was such at that time that it was ten years before Petrosian was ready to challenge Botvinnik for the world title.

By 1963, when Petrosian defeated Botvinnik, **FIDE** had removed the ex-champion's right to a revenge match, and Botvinnik didn't again attempt to qualify for world title contests.

Petrosian held the world championship from 1963 to 1969, when he lost to Boris Spassky.

From 1969 until his death in 1984 Petrosian entered many international events, among them the famous 1972 San Antonio tournament, where he shared first place with Karpov and Portisch.

Petrosian's play is best characterized as defensive. He preferred to play positionally, gaining space and controlling crucial squares rather than launching direct attacks. He also developed great skill in the endgame, which was well suited to his maneuvering style.

▼ **World champion for six years,** 1963–69, Petrosian had a defensive style of play and developed great skill in the endgame.

◄ **The Palace of the Young** Pioneers in Leningrad has been the training ground for the leading Soviet players of the postwar era. Here students from the palace take part in a display of simultaneous chess against Gary Kasparov (left), world champion since 1985.

Boris Spassky
(1937–   )

Spassky was born in Leningrad. As a child he studied chess for five hours every day at the Palace of the Young Pioneers, the traditional training ground for the leading Soviet players of the postwar era. He won the world junior championship in 1955 and the Soviet championship in 1961, but when he first challenged Petrosian for the world title in 1966, he lost. Three years later, on his next attempt, Spassky succeeded in taking Petrosian's crown.

Spassky's 1972 world title match against the American Bobby Fischer was one of the most publicized chess matches of modern times. The contest took place in Reykjavík, the capital city of Iceland, after a protracted series of negotiations in which the American came close to refusing to play.

The match itself was punctuated by Fischer's protests about the moves and the playing conditions. His demands included the exclusive use of the hotel swimming pool and a chessboard 3 millimeters smaller than that provided by the organizers. For his part, Spassky also came up with some unusual requests. After game 16, when Spassky was trailing 9½–6½, the Soviets asked for a complete investiga-

tion of the playing hall and its contents. They alleged that electronic devices or chemicals were being used to distract Spassky. A thorough investigation of the stage, walls, and lighting, and X rays of the players' chairs, revealed nothing more than two dead flies. The match continued, with the final score, 12½ –8½, signaling Spassky's defeat.

Spassky never recovered the form that had led him to the world throne. In 1978 he shared first place with World Champion Anatoly Karpov in a strong tournament held at Bugojno,

Bobby Fischer (1943–)

▲ **A cartoonist's impression of** the 1972 crowning ceremony in Reykjavík, when Fischer won the world title from Spassky (shown on Fischer's left).

Yugoslavia, and in 1983 was first at Linares, Spain, this time ahead of Karpov.

Spassky's chess style can be described as universal, in that he tackles all aspects of the game with equal skill and determination. He particularly enjoys launching daring attacks on his opponent's king, and as a beginner, you will find many of his games instructive in demonstrating this technique.

Amazingly, Fischer hasn't played a single game of chess in public since becoming world champion in 1972. He withdrew completely from the international chess circuit and now lives a reclusive life in California.

Fischer's mysterious lack of interest in competition chess is in sharp contrast to his early career. He learned to play when he was six and as a child read as many chess books as he could. At the age of 14 he became the chess champion of the United States and at 15 was the youngest ever **candidate** for the world championship. By the time he was 16 he was able to support himself financially through the game.

In 1962 Fischer created a sensation when he withdrew from international events. This was prompted by his fourth placing in the candidates' tournament in Curaçao, where he claimed that his Soviet opponents had cheated in order to prevent him from winning.

In 1967 Fischer pulled out of the Sousse **interzonal** after a dispute, thereby forfeiting the chance of playing for the world title for another three years. Finally, in 1970, he won the Palma de Mallorca interzonal with the phenomenal score of 18½, an astounding 3½ points ahead of the rest of the field.

Fischer then faced a series of candidates' matches to determine who should challenge Spassky for the title. In the first of these matches, against the Soviet **grandmaster** Mark Taimanov, Fischer did something almost unheard of in chess — he won every game (6–0). And he repeated this performance in the semi-final, against the Danish grandmaster Bent Larsen. The final match was against Petrosian, at that time the hardest player in the world to beat, but Fischer won the match by five games to one, with three draws.

Fischer's challenge match against Spassky in 1972 stimulated worldwide interest in chess on an unprecedented scale. Unfortunately, public attention centered on the negotiations away from the board and not on the chess, and many of Fischer's demands were misunderstood. Fischer hoped to achieve better conditions for all chess players, in regard to both the playing conditions (lighting, and so on) and the financial rewards (high prize money and appearance fees). In this respect there have been vast improvements since the 1970s, largely as a result of Fischer's efforts.

Fischer has also provided a lasting legacy of complex analysis of modern opening vari-ations, such as the Najdorf variation of the Sicilian defense. He is the author of *My 60 Memorable Games*, one of the classics of modern chess litera-ture, and his colorful career was the major inspiration for the musical, *Chess*.

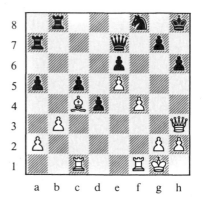

The position above is taken from the sixth game in the ex-hilarating 1972 world cham-pionship match between Fischer and Spassky. Before this game, the scores in the match were even.

Watch how Fischer (White) crashes through on the king's side of the board.

26.	f4 – f5!	e6 × f5
27.	Rf1 × f5	Nf8 – h7
28.	Rc1 – f1	Qe7 – d8
29.	Qh3 – g3	Ra7 – e7
30.	h2 – h4	Rb8 – b7
31.	e5 – e6	Rb7 – c7
32.	Qg3 – e5	Qd8 – e8
33.	a2 – a4	Qe8 – d8
34.	Rf1 – f2	Qd8 – e8

Spassky (Black) can only move

his queen back and forth, watching helplessly as Fischer's attack gains in force with every move.

35. Rf2 – f3	Qe8 – d8
36. Bc4 – d3	Qd8 – e8
37. Qe5 – e4	Nh7 – f6
38. Rf5 × f6!	g7 × f6
39. Rf3 × f6	Kh8 – g8
40. Bd3 – c4	Kg8 – h8
41. Qe4 – f4	Black resigns

Resigning was the only way to stop the move 42. Rf6–f8+ is 41. ... Kh8–g8, to which Fischer would have replied Qf4×h6.

▼ **World champion for ten years** until beaten by Gary Kasparov in 1985, Anatoly Karpov also has the distinction of having been awarded the chess oscar an unprecedented nine times.

Anatoly Karpov (1951–   )

Karpov learned to play chess when he was four and later studied with Botvinnik in Moscow and with Grandmaster Semyon Furman in Riga. He won the world junior championship in 1969, three points ahead of the other players, and only a year later gained his **grandmaster** title at a tournament in Caracas, Venezuela.

In 1973 Karpov won the Leningrad **interzonal** tournament and with it the chance to play in the **candidates'** matches to select Fischer's challenger. He defeated Polugayevsky,

Spassky, and Korchnoi in these matches, thereby earning the right to compete against the brilliant American.

Fischer drew up a list of conditions for the 1975 match with Karpov. Some of these were accepted but not all, and Fischer refused to play unless all his demands were met. **FIDE** held a special meeting to discuss the problem, but no solution was found. When Fischer formally refused to play the match, FIDE declared that he had lost his crown.

Karpov thus became the first champion to win by default. But it was soon evident that his name will go down in chess history as one of the greatest champions. His results since 1975 have been formidable, with more major tournament victories than any of his predecessors.

In 1978 and 1981 he successfully defended his title against Victor Korchnoi (who defected from the U.S.S.R. in 1976 and took up residence in the Netherlands). Between 1973 and 1984 Karpov was awarded the chess **oscar** an unprecedented nine times.

In playing style, Karpov is quiet but deadly accurate. At the board he is both determined and patient, often winning positions that appear to be tending toward a draw. The essence of his play lies in demonstrating that small advantages can be decisive in the correct hands.

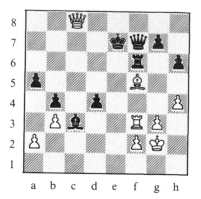

The position above shows the final phase of one of Karpov's wins against Gary Kasparov, in the fourth game of their 1985 match for the world championship.

Karpov played White in this game and Kasparov, Black.

57.	Qc8 – c5 +	Ke7 – e8
58.	Rf3 – f4	Qf7 – b7 +
59.	Rf4 – e4 +	Ke8 – f7

If Kasparov plays . . . Rf6–e6 in his 59th move instead, Karpov would play 60. Qc5–c4 followed by Qc4–g8 + .

60.	Qc5 – c4 +	Kf7 – f8
61.	Bf5 – h7	Rf6 – f7
62.	Qc4 – e6	Qb7 – d7
63.	Qe6 – e5	Black resigns

If Kasparov plays 63. . . . Qd7 –d8, it would be followed by 64. Qe5–c5 + Rf7–e7, 65. Re4–f4 + Kf8–e8, 66. Qc5–c6 + Qd8–d7, and then 67. Bh7–g6 + . Alternatively, 63. . . . Rf7–e7 would be followed by 64. Qe5–f4 + Re7–f7, 65. Qf4–b8 + . In both cases, Karpov wins easily.

Gary Kasparov (1963–   )

Kasparov's rise to world champion was astonishingly rapid. He became a **grandmaster** in 1980, at the extraordinarily young age of 17, and within two years was rated as the second strongest player in the world. In November 1985, age 22, he became the youngest world champion in the history of the title.

Kasparov's path to the world championship contained a number of formidable obstacles, both on the board and away from it. His 1983 **candidates'** match against the Soviet defector Victor Korchnoi was originally awarded to Korchnoi by default when the Soviet Chess Federation refused to allow Kasparov to play in California.

Korchnoi graciously agreed that the match could be played in London, and Kasparov won convincingly despite losing the first game. Kasparov won the next two qualifying matches and in 1984 was ready to face Karpov, who had held the throne for almost a decade.

Between 1984 and 1987 Kasparov played four matches against Karpov for the title. The 1984 match was abandoned in mid-play after five and a half months and 48 games, 40 of them drawn. The match was

▼ **Gary Kasparov (right) played** two championship matches against Anatoly Karpov (left) before wresting the world title from him in 1985.

КАРПОВ КАСПАРОВ

▲ **When Gary Kasparov won** the world championship in November 1985, he was only 22 years old – the youngest champion in the history of the title.

terminated by the president of **FIDE**, Florencio Campomanes of the Philippines, on the grounds that it had exhausted both the players and the organizers. Karpov had scored five wins and Kasparov three, two of which came in games 47 and 48. Controversy still surrounds the FIDE president's decision, and many chess fans felt that he stopped the match just as Kasparov had discovered the secret of beating Karpov.

To prevent another war of attrition, the 1985 match was limited to 24 games. This time Kasparov won by a score of 13 to 11 games.

Following his defeat, Karpov was granted the right to a revenge match. This began in London in July 1986 and marked the centenary of the first world championship match between Steinitz and Zukertort. Kasparov won this revenge match by 12½ to 11½, after one of the most exciting contests in history. Three points ahead after 16 games, Kasparov then lost three games in a row and only clinched the match with a sparkling win in the 22nd game.

In 1987 the two chess gladiators met yet again, this time in the Spanish town of Seville. The match was drawn, 12 points to each player, so Kasparov retains his title until at least 1990.

Kasparov is renowned for his fiery and energetic style at the chessboard, based on the styles of both Alekhine and Botvinnik. His personal attitude to the game is summed up by his comment: "Although chess contains elements of sport and science, for me it is primarily an art." Kasparov has shown that he in-

tends to popularize chess by playing in events that attract a wide public audience, and he has stated his determination to carry on and expand the work of the chess school founded by Botvinnik.

The position below shows the final stage of game 11 in the 1985 world championship match in Moscow between Kasparov and Karpov. Kasparov is White and Karpov, Black.

23. Qg4 × d7!!

A stunning queen sacrifice, and a move that Karpov had completely overlooked.

23. ...	Rd8 × d7
24. Re1 – e8 +	Kg8 – h7
25. Bd5 – e4 +	Black resigns

A most dramatic finale. After 25. . . . g7–g6, 26. Rd1 × d7 Bb7 –a6 and 27. Be4 × c6 Qf6 × c6, 28. Rd7 × f7 is checkmate.

▶ **The position before** White's 23rd move in game 11 of the 1985 world championship match in Moscow. Kasparov is White and Karpov is Black.

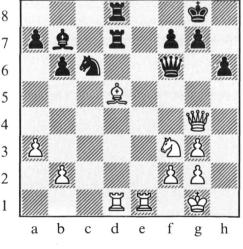

Women World Champions

A women's world championship has been held since 1927, and there have been three outstanding holders of the women's world title — Menchik, Gaprindashvili, and Chiburdanidze.

Vera Menchik was born in Moscow in 1906 and was the first woman to hold the world title. Her father was Czech and her mother British, and in 1921 the family settled in England where Vera studied with the Hungarian grandmaster Géza Maróczy. She became a chess professional, lecturing and giving displays and lessons. In international events she defeated a number of notable opponents, including Euwe and Reshevsky. Her chess career ended abruptly in 1944 when, together with her sister and mother, she was killed during an air raid on London.

Born in Tbilisi in Soviet Georgia in 1941, Nona Gaprindashvili held the world title for 16 years. She is an international **grandmaster**. This is primarily a men's title and one that very few women have obtained. She has also scored well in male-dominated international events, sharing first place in the American Lone Pine tournament in 1977. She and I shared second place in the 1978 Dortmund tournament.

Maya Chiburdanidze was born in 1961 and is the first female player to have been described as a child prodigy. She was awarded the title of international **master** in 1974, thus becoming the youngest player of either sex to receive a **FIDE** title. Since winning the women's world championship in 1978, she has achieved good results in a number of international tournaments. Together with the remarkable Polgar sisters of Hungary, she is now proving that chess is no longer a game dominated by men.

1927–1944	Vera Menchik	England
1950–1953	Ludmila Rudenko	U.S.S.R.
1953–1956	Elizaveta Bykova	U.S.S.R.
1956–1958	Olga Rubtsova	U.S.S.R.
1958–1962	Elizaveta Bykova	
1962–1978	Nona Gaprindashvili	U.S.S.R.
1978–	Maya Chiburdanidze	U.S.S.R.

▲ **Vera Menchik**
playing in a local
tournament at
Margate, England,
in 1935. She had
been world
champion for eight
years.

▶ **Chiburdanidze**
has held the
women's world title
since 1978. Here
she is in 1984
wearing the laurel
wreath of the world
champion, which
she had just won
for the third
successive time.

8: Computers & Chess

The first attempts at designing chess-playing machines had more to do with the realm of magic and illusion than with pure science. The earliest of these machines was the Turk, an automaton that was exhibited by the Hungarian engineer and inventor Baron Wolfgang von Kempelen at the Viennese Royal Palace in 1769. The baron was the counselor on mechanics to the court, and he was famous for his mechanical genius. His new invention was contained within a chest roughly 4 feet long, 1½ feet wide, and 3 feet high. There was a chessboard on the top of the chest and the pieces were kept in a drawer at the bottom. Behind the chest sat a life-size mechanical figure dressed as a Turk (see the engraving top right).

Von Kempelen claimed that the Turk could play chess. After winding it up with a key, he would invite members of the audience to come forward and play against the automaton. To the accompanying whirr of clockwork, the Turk would pick up a piece in its left hand and slowly move it to a new square.

At the beginning and end of the exhibition the baron would allow members of the audience to examine the machine, but no one discovered its secret. The Turk was in fact an elaborate illusion: a human operator was hidden in a concealed compartment inside it.

Two later devices, Ajeeb and Mephisto, both worked on similar principles.

It was not until the late 19th century that the first genuine chess-playing machine was developed. The Spanish scientist Torre y Quevedo's mechanism played the ending king and rook against king, always taking the side with the rook and always forcing checkmate. Quevedo's machine is still in working order and can be seen in Madrid's museum of polytechnics.

Little progress in automated chess was made until the 1940s, when Alan Turing in England and Claude Shannon in the United States outlined their ideas on programming computers to play the game. A decade later, in 1958, the first computer chess program was operational in the United States.

By 1970 there were sufficient programs for a chess tournament to be possible in which all of the contestants were computer programs. Interest in the subject grew quickly, and in 1974 the first world computer chess championship took place

▲ ▶ The chess-playing machine has come a long way in 200 years. Invented by Baron von Kempelen in the 1760s, the Turk (above) was an elaborate hoax — a human operator was concealed inside it. It may still seem like magic to most of us, but the microchip is the only hidden component of the modern chess computer.

in Stockholm, Sweden, attracting 13 entries. The winner was the Soviet program KAISSA, written at the Institute of Control Science in Moscow.

The world computer chess championship is now held regularly every three years, and since KAISSA all the winners have been programs written in the United States.

Early attempts at programming concentrated on the "brute force" approach, in which the computer searched most variations to the same depth, examining millions of positions in its attempt to find the best moves. It is well known

▲ **The world's first computer** chess championship was held in Stockholm in 1974. The winner was the Soviet program KAISSA, written at Moscow's Institute of Control Science.

now, however, that strong human players do not play chess in this way. Such players tend to consider a very small number of moves, sometimes analyzing one or two variations to a greater depth than in the early computer programs. Experience tells the human chess master that in some positions no more than two or three moves will be playable. As a result of these findings, the more recent work on computer chess has centered increasingly on the "selective search" approach, in which the computer looks at a smaller number of moves, concentrating on the ones that are most useful and interesting.

Most of the major research into computer chess has been undertaken by experts in the United States, the Soviet Union, and Britain. In the U.S.S.R., former world champion Mikhail Botvinnik has been actively involved in this work. He believes that the problem of teaching a computer to play good chess "can be solved only by chess specialists using their creative experience." Despite Botvinnik's enthusiasm for the subject, many strong players remain doubtful about the prospects of developing a computer program that can play chess to a world-class level.

In 1968 David Levy, who was to become an international **master** a year later, wagered that no computer program would be able to beat him within ten years. In 1978 he won the bet by defeating the then world champion program, CHESS 4.7, in a match in Toronto, Canada. Levy had worked on computer chess himself and understood the problems involved in the task of writing a strong chess program. He was confident from the outset that he would win his bet.

The main weaknesses of current chess programs are due to their inability to plan and to

▼ **In 1968 David Levy wagered** that no one would be able to write a computer program capable of beating him within ten years. In 1978 he defeated the then world champion program and won his bet.

their relatively weak grasp of strategic concepts. Tactically, however, computers are very advanced and can examine some forced variations at a much greater depth than human beings can. Computers are thus able to play certain endgames with total accuracy. Recently an American computer programmer, Ken Thompson, put all the positions for the ending king and queen against king and rook on computer disk. In total, the positions number about four million. Thompson's program demonstrated that no winning line took more than 31 moves and that the computer could therefore play this ending much more skillfully than a number of human **masters** and **grandmasters**.

The ultimate aim for computer chess experts lies in con-structing a program that can beat the human world chess champion. This goal is still a long way off, despite the fact that a number of grandmasters have been defeated in five-minute chess by computer programs, while Professor Hans Berliner's program HITECH has won matches against a number of strong players, including the prominent female grandmaster Dr. Jana Miles.

Computer experts believe that writing chess programs can help us to learn about the ways in which chess players think. A further spin-off is the insight such knowledge can give into the development of programming techniques for use in other spheres, such as long-range planning and military research (HITECH is partly funded by the United States Air Force). It is not beyond the bounds of belief that the basic techniques for constructing a humanoid robot capable of thinking for itself — like C-3PO in the film *Star Wars* — could arise from intensive work in programming machines to master the logical processes needed for playing chess.

The following game demonstrates the power of HITECH, the computer program that beat Dr. Jana Miles in a two-game match in London in 1986. HITECH is White, and Black is Jana Miles. They are playing a variation of the Caro–Kann defense (see also, pages 75–76).

▼ **The battle between humans** and computers is now well under way. Sixteen-year-old Theresa Needham scored a point for the human side when she won the Computer Chess Challenger national tournament in London in 1982.

1.	e2 – e4	c7 – c6
2.	d2 – d4	d7 – d5
3.	Nb1 – c3	g7 – g6
4.	h2 – h3	Bf8 – g7
5.	Ng1 – f3	Ng8 – h6
6.	e4 × d5	c6 × d5
7.	Bf1 – b5 +	Bc8 – d7
8.	Bc1 × h6	Bg7 × h6
9.	Qd1 – e2	0–0

An unsound pawn **sacrifice** on Black's part. A better move for Miles is . . . Bd7–c6.

10.	Nc3 × d5	Bd7 × b5
11.	Qe2 × b5	Nb8 – c6
12.	c2 – c3	a7 – a6
13.	Qb5 – c5	Ra8 – c8
14.	0–0	e7 – e6

If Miles plays 14. . . . Nc6 × d4 instead, then 15. Qc5 × c8! Qd8 × c8 and 16. Nd5 × e7 + would follow, with HITECH **forking** the black king and queen.

15.	Nd5 – b6	Rc8 – c7
16.	Qc5 – a3	Bh6 – f4
17.	Rf1 – e1	Nc6 – e7
18.	c3 – c4	Ne7 – f5
19.	Ra1 – d1	Qd8 – f6
20.	d4 – d5	

Black has no compensation and the pawn advance is decisive.

20.	. . .	Bf4 – d6
21.	b2 – b4	a6 – a5
22.	Qa3 × a5	Qf6 – c3
23.	a2 – a3	e4 × d5
24.	Nb6 × d5	Qc3 × c4
25.	Nd5 × c7	Bd6 × c7
26.	Qa5 – c5	Qc4 – f4
27.	Rd1 – d7	Bd6 – b8
28.	Re1 – d1	b7 – b6
29.	Qc5 × b6	Nf5 – h4

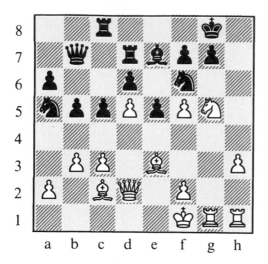

◀ The position after Black's 27th move in the 1985 game between World Champion Gary Kasparov and the chess computer Mephisto. Kasparov was White.

A move made in desperation, for Miles has no real attack.

30. Nf3 × h4	Qf4 – h2 +
31. Kg1 – f1	Qh2 – h1 +
32. Kf1 – e2	Rf8 – e8 +
33. Ke2 – f3	Qh1 – h2
34. Qb6 – f6	Black resigns

This was the first time a computer had beaten a grandmaster under tournament conditions. The rate of play was 40 moves in two hours.

We'll now take a look at the sacrificial masterpiece played by World Champion Gary Kasparov against the chess computer Mephisto. The game was played in 1985 in Hamburg, West Germany, during a **blindfold** exhibition in which Kasparov played ten games simultaneously without sight of the boards. We join the game after Black's 27th move. Kasparov is White and Mephisto, Black.

From this position (see the board above), Kasparov now indulges in a series of **sacrifices**, which open up his opponent's position and lead to a checkmating trap.

28. Ng5 – e6!	f7 × e6
29. f5 × e6	Rd7 – c7
30. Rg1 × g7 + !!	Kg8 × g7
31. Be3 – h6 +	Kg7 – h8
32. Bh6 – g7 + !	

This decisive third sacrifice opens the way for the white queen to join the fray.

32. . . .	Kh8 × g7
33. Qd2 – g5 +	Kg7 – f8
34. Qg5 – h6 +	Kf8 – e8
35. Bc2 – g6 +	Ke8 – d8
36. Qh6 – h8 +	Black resigns

Contact your local chess association for information about companies that are able to supply chess computers.

9: Tournament Tips

Once you have mastered the basics of chess, a good way to improve your game is by playing in clubs and tournaments. Playing with friends at home is, of course, quite different from playing at club level. Certain formalities have to be observed in club or tournament chess, but these are easy to follow and in the long run will add to your enjoyment of the game.

Tournaments are run by arbiters or controllers. These officials are always ready to advise new players about the rules and regulations of chess. Remember, however, that it is against the rules to ask anyone for advice about which moves to play on the board when a game is in progress.

Keeping Score

If you enter a tournament you will be expected to keep an accurate record of the moves of the game on a **score sheet**. This can be employed to verify the moves if a dispute arises. The score sheet is also a valuable personal record, which you can use to replay the game at your leisure to see where your moves could be improved.

To keep score you need to be familiar with **algebraic notation** (see chapter 2) and be able to note down the moves correctly. Practice at home when playing friendly games and by reading

▲ **Players in tournament chess** record the moves of the game on score sheets.

chess books — you'll discover that you'll soon be able to record your games with ease.

Clocks

At club and tournament level you will be expected to use a chess clock. This is a device with two clock faces — one shows the amount of time used by White and the other the time used by Black. While one clock is running, the other is stopped.

The clocks are usually started

by a button or a switch. While you are thinking about a move your clock should be running. Once you have made your move you should press your button or switch to stop your side of the clock and start your opponent's clock.

The clocks ensure that games proceed on schedule and that each player has the same amount of time as the other to make moves. During the 19th century, before the chess clocks were introduced, games could run on forever.

▼ **Chess clocks are used in** tournament chess to ensure that games proceed on schedule. Here, Capablanca studies the board at a tournament at Margate, England, in 1935.

Time Limit

If you are using a chess clock you will be expected to make a set number of moves within a certain time. A common time limit in international play is 40 moves within two and a half hours. This means that the first session lasts a maximum of five hours, and during that time each player must make 40 moves. More moves can be played, but many players prefer to stop at the 40th move so that they can think about their position during the break.

In cases when the game hasn't finished after five hours, there is a break and then a shorter second session.

The Sealed Move

If the game is unfinished at the end of a session, one player will "seal" a move. This means that the player decides on his or her next move and writes it on the **score sheet** — the move is not played on the chessboard.

The score sheet is then placed in a sealed envelope to be opened by the tournament controller at the start of the next session. The sealed move is not revealed to anyone until the game resumes.

Adjudication

For practical reasons, it is sometimes impossible to finish a game that is part of a club match or tournament. You might be part of a school team playing at another school many miles away, for instance, with a fixed time for play so that you can all get home at a reasonable hour.

To allow a fair result to be achieved if for some reason a game is unfinished, an adjudicator, or judge, can be called in. This must be someone who is a very strong player. The adjudicator must assess what the result of the game would be if both players were to continue in the correct way. It can often take the adjudicator hours to work

on a position, analyzing it in detail to find the correct result.

Speed Chess

Sometimes the time limit is very short. The players might be required to make all their moves in 30 minutes or even 5 minutes,

for example. These fast rates of play often result in some very exciting chess. A good example of this is the match that took place in London early in 1987, between World Champion Gary Kasparov and the top British player, Nigel Short. Each player was permitted 25 minutes per game to complete all moves.

Kasparov won by four games

▲ **World Champion Gary** Kasparov (left) and Grandmaster Nigel Short playing speed chess in 1987. Each of them was allowed just 25 minutes in which to complete his moves in each game of the tense encounter.

to two. The play was enthralling and attracted over one million viewers when it was telecast.

10: Finding Out More

Your local library should be able to help you find the nearest chess clubs to where you live. If your library cannot assist you, contact your national chess federation.

Contact Addresses

The U.S. Chess Federation is the governing board of U.S. chess players of the World Chess Federation. It conducts all championship events, including the National Open, U.S. Championship, U.S. Junior, U.S. Open, and U.S. Women's. The federation sends teams abroad to compete in international chess tournaments, and maintains a rating system for every U.S. chess tournament. This rating system, which rates players on a scale of 0 to 3000, is considered one of the best sports rating systems in the world.

The Canadian Chess Federation is the governing body of Canadian chess, and organizes championship events in that country.

United States Chess Federation
186 Route 9W
New Windsor, NY 12550
(914) 562–8350

Canadian Chess Federation
Box 7339
Ottawa, Ontario
Canada
K11 8E

Different associations exist in order to promote other chess programs, including correspondence chess, chess in schools, and chess for the blind, for the deaf and for senior citizens. You can obtain details of these associations and other specialist groups from the above addresses.

Major Tournaments

Since 1900, an open national chess tournament has been held annually in the United States. Today, there are 22 U.S. national tournaments and around 5000 regional and local tournaments held throughout the United States. These tournaments are open to players of all ages. The U.S. Chess Federation also sponsors tournaments especially for young people. The U.S. Junior Open and the National Scholastic Tournaments (National Elementary, National Junior High, and National High School) do not require qualification. For more information, contact the U.S. Chess Federation.

In Canada, there is one major national tournament, the Canadian Open. The Keres Memorial in British Columbia and the Toronto Labor Day Tournament are two popular regional events. For more information, contact the Canadian Chess Federation.

▼ **The final tournament of the**
British chess championships
takes place in August each year.
It includes sections for players of
all strengths and all ages

Further Reading

Of all the board games, chess has by far the most extensive literature. There are books on general opening theory, there are books on specific openings, and there are even monographs on single opening variations. Numerous studies of the middle game and the endgame have been published, as well as biographies of the greatest players, books on individual tournaments and matches, and, of course, histories of the game itself.

Many of the chess classics are still in print, but local libraries are the best hunting grounds for books that are out of print. Second-hand bookshops are also often a good source for older works and are a cheap way of building up a personal chess library.

All of the books mentioned in chapter 7, on the world champions, will repay the time you invest in studying them. The following recommended works will also take you a stage further in your development as a chess player.

Alekhine, A. *My Best Games 1908–1923* and *My Best Games 1924–1937* (Dover). These two classic works have been reprinted in one volume.

Eales, R. *Chess: The History of a Game* (Facts on File).

Fischer, R. *Bobby Fischer Teaches Chess* (Bantam).

Karpov, A. *Chess at the Top: 1979–1984* (Pergamon).

Kasparov, G. *Fighting Chess: My Games & Career* (Collets, U.K.). Kasparov's own collection of his games.

Kasparov, G. *The World Chess Championship Match—Moscow 1985* (Pergamon).

Keres, P. *Keres' Best Games of Chess: 1931–1948* (Dover).

Keres, P. *Practical Chess Endings* (Batsford). A useful guide to ideas and strategies in the endgame.

Levy, D. & Newborn, M. *All About Chess & Computers* (Computer Science).

Nimzowitsch, A. *My System* (McKay). A classic work and still the most stimulating book on the middle game.

Newspaper columns and magazines

Most major newspapers, including the *New York Times*, *Los Angeles Times*, *Boston Globe*, and *San Francisco Chronicle*, carry a regular chess column. In Canada, the *Globe & Mail*, *Toronto Star*, *Ottawa Citizen*, *Winnepeg Press*, and *La Presse*, Montreal have chess columns.

There are also numerous magazines which are dedicated solely to chess. The U.S. Chess Federation publishes *Chess Life*, a monthly magazine for members, and also *Schoolmates*, a chess magazine for young people that comes out four times a year. For information, contact the U.S. Chess Federation at the address given on page 174. Another national magazine is *Inside Chess* published twice a month in Seattle, WA. This magazine carries instructional articles and articles about international events. For subscription information, write or call I.C.E. Inc., Box 19457, Seattle, WA., 98109, (206) 723-6924.

In Canada, the Canadian Chess Federation publishes *En Passant*, which comes out every other month.

Glossary

Not all of the following terms have been employed in this book, but you will find them useful in helping you to understand more advanced chess books that you may read in the future.

Algebraic notation
A system of abbreviation used to record the moves of a chess game. Algebraic notation is based on a grid of eight letters (a–h) for the files and eight numbers (1–8) for the ranks. *See also* chapter 2.

Backward pawn
A pawn that has been left behind by its neighbors and can no longer rely on their support. *See also* page 100.

Bad bishop
A bishop that is trapped behind its own pawns, which are on squares the same color as itself. *See also* page 102.

Blindfold chess
A game played without sight of the board. Blindfold players must keep the position in their heads and call out their moves in chess notation. Their opponents must also call out their moves. Some chess masters can play a number of different chess games blindfold at the same time.

Candidate
A player who has qualified to compete for the right to play the world champion for the title. The candidates' matches are the final eliminating stage of the competition to decide the world champion's opponent in the title match.

Capture
To capture, a player must make a legal move that lands a piece on a square containing an enemy piece. The captured enemy piece is taken from the board and removed from the game. *See also* En passant.

Castling
A maneuver in which the king and a rook are moved simultaneously. Both pieces must be in their starting positions and the path to their new squares must not be blocked by another piece. *See also* pages 48–49.

Check
A move that attacks the enemy king.

Checkmate (mate)
The end of the game, when a player's king is threatened with certain capture and cannot

escape the check. *See also* pages 56–60.

Closed file
A file that has a white pawn and a black pawn stationed on it. *See also* page 101.

Closed positions
Chess positions in which there are blocked pawn chains.

Combination
A forcing sequence of moves with an advantageous goal, often involving the sacrifice of material.

Correspondence chess
See Postal chess.

▲ **The candidates' matches are** the final eliminating stage of the competition to decide the world champion's opponent in the match for the title.

Development
The process of bringing out pieces to squares where they are performing some useful function. *See also* chapter 4, "The Opening."

Discovered check
A check that occurs when one piece is moved out of the path of another piece, enabling the second piece to give check. See the example of this type of check in game 1 on pages 58–59.

Double check

A move that is a discovered check, and in which the piece that moves also gives check. The only way out of a double check is to move the king — you cannot block both checking pieces, nor can you make a move that would capture them both at once. See the example on page 94.

Doubled pawns

Two pawns of the same color positioned one in front of the other on the same file. *See also* page 95.

Draw

The result of a game in which neither side wins. In competition chess, half a point is awarded to each player. For the various ways in which a game can be drawn, see pages 107–10.

En passant

A special type of pawn capture. If a pawn advances two squares on its first move and lands on a square adjacent to an enemy pawn, then the enemy pawn can capture the advancing pawn on the next move of the game — as though the advancing pawn had moved only one square forward. *See also* page 31.

En prise

A piece is said to be en prise if it can be captured for nothing, or for insufficient compensation. Any piece that is being attacked but which isn't defended is en prise. A defended piece that is under attack from one less valuable than itself is also en prise — for example, a defended queen that is being attacked by a rook.

Equality (equal position)

A balanced chess position in which both players have the same chance of winning.

Exchange, the

To gain or lose a rook (a major piece) for a bishop or a knight (minor pieces).

Exchange, to

To trade, or swap, pieces of equal value (see "Values of the Pieces," page 45). If White captures a black bishop, for example, Black then captures a white knight or bishop.

Fianchetto

A maneuver in which a knight's pawn (the b-pawn or the g-pawn) is advanced one square and the bishop developed behind it. For example, White could start the game by playing 1. g2–g3 and 2. Bf1–g2, which would fianchetto his king's bishop. This bishop would then be referred to as a "fianchettoed bishop." The value of the move is that it places the bishop on the longest diagonal of the board (a8–h1 or a1–h8).

FIDE

Fédération Internationale des Échecs (International Chess

Federation), founded in Paris in 1924. The world's governing body for chess, and the organization that determines the rules for the game and controls world championship events and the awarding of titles such as international master and international grandmaster.

Files
The vertical columns of squares on a chessboard.

Flank
One side of the chessboard (queen's side or king's side).

Fork
A move that attacks more than one enemy piece. *See also* the examples on pages 103–104.

Gambit
An opening or variation in which material is sacrificed in order to achieve rapid piece development. Most gambits involve the sacrifice of one or two pawns, but there are a few gambits in which a minor piece is sacrificed. See, for example, the openings on pages 81–86.

Good bishop
A mobile bishop — one that isn't impeded by its own pawns on the same color squares as itself. *See also* page 102.

Grandmaster
A title awarded by FIDE for consistently good play in international events. The full title is international grandmaster,

▶ **The title of** grandmaster is awarded by FIDE for consistently good play in international events. The British player Nigel Short was only 19 when he was awarded the title in 1984.

which is rather a mouthful. At present there are about three hundred grandmasters in the world. *See also* Master.

Hanging pawns
Two pawns in neighboring files, which are neither passed nor opposed by an enemy pawn on the same file. *See also* pages 98–99.

Illegal move
A move that does not conform to the rules of chess — usually a move into check, or one that fails to get a king out of check. The most frequently made illegal moves are probably those executed by players who do not fully understand the castling rules.

Initiative
Having the initiative means that your opponent is on the run. You have been making moves that carry immediate or subtle threats, and your opponent has been forced on the defensive. If you can keep up the initiative with accurate play, and if you don't allow your opponent any breathing space in which to launch a counter offensive, you will have a good chance of winning the game.

Interzonal
The interzonal tournaments are the qualifying stage for the candidates' matches. They were established by FIDE in 1947.

Isolated pawn
A pawn that isn't supported by pawns on the files adjacent to it. *See also* pages 96–97.

King's side
The side of the chessboard on which the king is positioned at the start of the game (for White, the right-hand flank). Pieces positioned on this side of the board are known as the king's bishop, king's knight, and king's rook.

Legal move
A move permitted by the rules of chess — note that this is not necessarily a good move.

Lone king
When a player has only a king remaining on the board. See pages 123–28 for endgame strategy involving a lone king.

Major piece
A queen or a rook.

Master
Another title awarded by FIDE, but for players who are not yet of grandmaster strength. The full title is international master.

Mate
See Checkmate.

Material
The value of a player's chess pieces. The player with an advantage in material, or who is "ahead on material," has a total

piece value greater than that of his or her opponent. If a pawn is counted as one unit of strength, then a queen is worth nine pawns, a rook is worth five, and bishops and knights, three pawns each. *See also* page 45.

Minor piece
A knight or a bishop.

Mobility
The freedom of action of the chess pieces, measured by the number of squares a player's pieces are attacking, including those occupied by enemy pieces. *See also* page 92.

Odds
Giving an advantage at the start of the game, to compensate for the difference in strength between the two players. Giving and receiving odds was very popular during the 19th century and earlier, when masters would give anything from a pawn (usually the f-pawn) to a queen or more (the chosen piece is removed from the board before play starts). Nowadays, giving material odds in this way is rather rare, but the advent of the chess clock has made it possible for strong players to give time odds — taking one or two minutes for all their moves, for example, and allowing their opponents five minutes or more.

Open file
A file on which there are no pawns of either color. *See also* page 101.

Open positions
Chess positions in which the center of the chessboard is usually clear of pawns, and where both sides' pieces have great freedom of movement.

Opposition, the
Whenever the kings face each other on the same file, with only one square between them, the player who made the last move is said to have the opposition. *See also* page 112.

Oscar
An award presented by the International Association of the Chess Press. The first chess oscar was awarded in 1967 to Bent Larsen, the Danish grandmaster.

Passed pawn
A pawn whose forward march cannot be stopped by an enemy pawn, either on the same or an adjacent file. *See also* page 98.

Pawn center
A position in which pawns occupy more than one of the central squares d4, d5, e4, e5.

Pawn chain
A position in which a number of pawns of the same color are placed diagonally across adjacent files, thus protecting each other from enemy attack.

Pawn majority
The player who has the greater number of pawns on one side of the board is said to have a pawn majority on that flank. *See also* pages 118–19.

Perpetual check
A position when one of the players can give check move after move after move. *See also* pages 109–10.

Pin, pinned
A pin is when one piece (the pinned piece) is shielding a more valuable piece from enemy attack and therefore cannot move. *See also* page 105.

Postal chess
Also known as correspondence chess, this is when a game is played by mail. White records his first move in chess notation and mails it to Black. Within a few days of receiving this move, Black works out her reply, writes it down, and sends it back. There are national and international competitions for postal players, in addition to a world correspondence chess championship, which is recognized by FIDE.

Problem
A composed position, in which one side (normally White) must force mate within a specific number of moves, against any defense. Creating such problems is an art, and there are even problem-composing tour-

184

naments in which the competitors try to create "beautiful" problems. There are also problem-solving competitions in which the aim is to find the solutions as quickly as possible.

Promotion
When a pawn reaches its 8th rank, it is promoted immediately to become a queen, rook, bishop, or knight — whatever the player who owns it chooses — but never a king. *See also* pages 32–33, and Underpromotion.

Queen's side
The side of the chessboard on which the queen is positioned at the start of the game (for Black, the right-hand flank) Pieces positioned on this side of the board are known as the queen's bishop, queen's rook, and queen's knight.

Rank
The horizontal rows of squares on a chessboard.

Resign
To resign a game is to admit defeat. A wise person once said that no one ever won a game by resigning. This is true, and while learning to play you should never resign, as your opponent might not know how to convert an enormous advantage into a win. But as you become more experienced you will normally resign when your position is hopeless and you think your opponent is strong enough to finish you off.

Sacrifice
The surrender of material in order to gain some advantage, such as an attack, superior mobility, or a larger amount of material.

Score sheet
The paper on which the moves of a game are recorded during play. *See also* page 170.

Semi-open file
A file with only one pawn on it (and possibly some pieces other than pawns). *See also* page 101.

Simultaneous exhibition
A display in which a strong chess player takes on a number of weaker players at the same time. The world record for the greatest number of participants in a simultaneous exhibition is 301 players. And the record for the most games played simultaneously by a chess master (who was playing all the games blindfold) is a staggering 62 games.

Skewer
An attack on two pieces, along the same rank, file, or diagonal. *See also* pages 104–105.

Smothered mate
A checkmating position which the attacking piece is knight and the enemy kin

hemmed in by its own pieces. For example:

1.	e2 – e4	e7 – e5
2.	f2 – f4	e5 × f4
3.	Ng1 – f3	g7 – g5
4.	Nb1 – c3	g5 – g4
5.	Nf3 – e5	Qd8 – h4 +
6.	g2 – g3	f4 × g3
7.	Qd1 × g4	g3 – g2 +
8.	Qg4 × h4	g2 × h1 = Q
9.	Qh4 – h5	Bf8 – e7
10.	Ne5 × f7	Ng8 – f6
11.	Nf7 – d6 +	Ke8 – d8
12.	Qh5 – e8 +	Rh8 × e8
13.	Nd6 – f7 checkmate	

The black king is smothered by its own pieces, as the board below shows.

Stalemate

A position when the player whose turn it is to move cannot make any legal moves but is not in check. It ends the game immediately as a draw. *See also* the examples on pages 61–63.

Study

A composed position in which the aim is not to force checkmate within a specified number of moves, as in a problem, but to achieve a more general goal, such as winning or drawing.

Tempo, tempi

A tempo is a move that can be thought of as a unit of time on the chessboard. You will understand what is meant by losing a tempo if you play these moves: 1. g2–g3 e7–e5; 2. Bf1–h3 d7 –d5; 3. Bh3–g2. White has lost a tempo because he moved his bishop from f1 to g2 in two moves when it could have reached the same square in just one move. Try to avoid wasting moves (or tempi), because it gives your opponent the chance to gain the initiative.

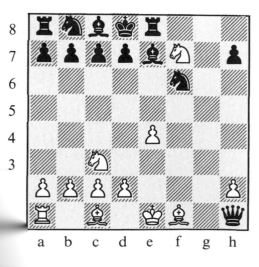

◄ **Smothered mate** occurs when the enemy king is hemmed in by its own pieces and the attacking piece is a knight, as in the position illustrated here.

▲ **In a simultaneous** exhibition, a strong player takes on a number of weaker players at the same time.

Touch-move rule
It is considered good manners in chess to move a piece once you have touched it. This is compulsory in competition chess.

Underpromotion
Promoting a pawn to a rook, bishop, or knight, rather than to a queen.

Wing
One side of the chessboard (queen's side or king's side).

Zugzwang
A position in which the player whose turn it is to move is at a disadvantage only because it is his or her turn to move, and for no other reason. For an example of zugzwang, see page 114 and the board illustrating the position after Black's sixth move. White is in zugzwang because he must move his king either to a square that brings about stalemate or to a square from which it no longer defends the pawn at d7. If it were Black's turn to move, White would win.

Zwischenzug
An intermediate move in an apparently forced sequence, usually conferring some kind of surprise advantage.

Index

Page numbers in **bold face** type refer to main entries in the Glossary; page numbers in *italic* type refer to illustrations.

A

adjudication   172
Ajeeb   162
Alekhine, Alexander   129, 137, 141–2, *141*, 143, 144, 159, 176
algebraic notation   18–20, *19*, 24, 26–7, 31, 32, 49, 170, **178**
Anderssen, Adolf   133, 134–6, *134*, 138
associations, chess   174
Austria, *see* Steinitz
automatons   162, *163*

B

bad bishop   102, *102*, **178**
backward pawn   100, *100*, **178**
Berliner, Professor Hans   166
bishop   37–8, 45
   see also bad bishop; good bishop; opposite-colored bishops
blindfold chess   130, *141*, 168, **178**
Boi, Paolo   130
Botvinnik, Mikhail   74, 75, 137, 144–6, *144*, 147, 148, 149, 155, 159, 165
Britain   8, 133, 165
   see also Levy; Menchik; Short; Staunton
Bykova, Elizaveta   160

C

Campomanes, Florencio   158

candidate   153, **178**, *179*
Capablanca, José   74, 137, 140, *140*, 141, 142, *143*, 144, *171*
capture   17, 20, 26, 29, 34, 38, 40, 41, 44, 45, 46, **178**
   see also en passant; en prise
Caro-Kann defense   75–6, 167–8
castling   48–51, *48*, 67, 92–3, **178**
Center Counter game   67
check   20, 47, 53–5, **178**
   see also checkmate; discovered check; double check; perpetual check
checkmate   16, 56–60, 122–8, **178–9**
   see also smothered mate
CHESS 4.7   165
chess clocks   170–1, *171*
chess notation, *see* algebraic notation
chess oscar, *see* oscar
chess pieces   6, *6, 7*, 8, *8–9*, 20, 28–47
Chess Player's Chronicle   133
chess programs, *see* CHESS 4.7; HITECH; KAISSA
chess sets   7, *12–13*, 13, 15, *89*
chess symbols   14, 24
Chiburdanidze, Maya   160, *161*
clocks, *see* chess clocks
closed file   101, *101*, **179**
closed positions   38, **179**
combination   **179**
computer chess   162–8, 176
Cook, Nathaniel   7
correspondence chess, *see* postal chess
Cuba, *see* Capablanca

ACKNOWLEDGMENTS

The publishers wish to thank the following for supplying photographs for this book:

Page 6 Michael Holford; 10 Macdonald/Aldus Archive (top and bottom); 11 Bridgeman Art Library; 12 Macdonald/Aldus Archive; 13 Macdonald/Aldus Archive (top), Topham (bottom); 16–17 Topham; 25 Pergamon Chess; 50 Mary Evans Picture Library; 55 Macdonald/Aldus Archive; 63 Macdonald/Aldus Archive; 78 Bridgeman Art Library; 80 Macdonald/Aldus Archive; 89 Topham; 99 Mary Evans Picture Library; 129 Fabio Biagi; 131 Mansell Collection; 132 Mansell Collection; 134 BBC Hulton Picture Library; 137 Mansell Collection; 139–143 BBC Hulton Picture Library; 144–151 Novosti Press Agency; 152–153 Macdonald/Aldus Archive; 155 Topham; 157 Novosti Press Agency; 158 Topham; 161 BBC Hulton Picture Library (top), Novosti Press Agency (bottom); 163 Mary Evans Picture Library (top), Computer Games Ltd (bottom); 164 Hans Svedbark; 165 Professor B Mittman; 167 Topham; 171 BBC Hulton Picture Library; 172–173 Thames Television; 175 Fabio Biagi; 179 Pergamon Chess; 181 Topham; 184 Topham.

Picture research by Sarah Donald

Studio photographs by Keith Rotherham Studio
Illustrations by Rhoda and Robert Burns